Praise for *Crooked Vows*

John Watt's *Crooked Vows* is not only a compulsive read, it is also an evocative, almost poetic survival story conjuring up the beauty, power and destructiveness of the West Australian bush, coast and the ocean. It is also a story of self-discovery. It vividly captures the struggles of a young man in the 1950s trying to come to terms with meaning, belief and sexuality within an abusive and claustrophobic Catholicism. The cleverly constructed plot contrasts survival in the wilderness after a plane crash and the recovery of suppressed memories, with the turgid boredom of 1950s' suburbia. The writing is limpid and engaging and tells the story with grace and elegance. It is a book that lingers in your memory.

—Dr Paul Collins, Writer, broadcaster and historian

Thomas's gradual emergence from a narrow dogmatic culture makes a fascinating story, cleverly constructed, in part through flashbacks to a series of overwhelming experiences. Lyrically written at times, it succeeds as a good mystery, unveiling its secrets in stages, but beneath that is a poetic quest for meaning and humanity in a world where a sexual predator is more acceptable than the one who exposes him.

—Dr Felicity Haynes, Philosopher,
former Dean of Education,
The University of Western Australia

Crooked Vows is a timely exploration of the dark and debilitating consequences of the Catholic Church's teaching on sexuality, desire and the body. Importantly, it recognises that damage is inflicted on both children and the family, as well as on the members of its ordained clergy. Framed by the story of a trainee priest's attempts to recover memories of the days following a plane crash, the novel cleverly integrates bush and city, guilt and desire, psychology and faith in a surprisingly suspenseful narrative.

—Robyn Cadwallader, Blogger,
Writer for Verity La Journal

Offered to us as a tale of turmoil in a Catholic soul, John Watt's novel is also a deeply-felt study of the human struggle for liberty; of the price we might be willing to pay, and why we should.

—Robert Hillman, Award-winning author
with over 60 published works

This novel serves as a timely and sensitive portrayal of the struggles of a young would-be priest struggling to come to terms with his sexuality and beliefs inside the strictures of a Church shackled to centuries of tradition and dogma. Set partly in South West of Western Australia, its plot hinges on a mysterious tale of survival in the wilderness and repressed memories. Yet what lingers long after reading is a sadder, more tempered understanding of the horrific human toll of those strictures of 1950s' Catholicism—a toll that is yet to reach its full accounting.

—Bron Sibree, Journalist and reviewer

CROOKED VOWS

JOHN WATT

WILD
DINGO
PRESS

Published by Wild Dingo Press
Melbourne, Australia
books@wilddingopress.com.au
www.wilddingopress.com.au

First published by Wild Dingo Press 2016.

Cover design: Gisela Beer
Cover photos: Kerrilyn Boase-Jelinek
Layout: Midland Typesetters, Australia
Editor: Katia Ariel
Printed in Australia by Ligare

National Library in Australia
Cataloguing-in-Publications Data

Watt, John, 1936-
Crooked Vows / John Watt
First edition.

ISBN: 9780987381187 (paperback)
ISBN: 9780987381194 (eBook)

Seminarians—Western Australia—Fiction.
Faith—Fiction.
Belief and doubt—Fiction.
Clergy—Conduct of life—Fiction.
Sexual misconduct by clergy—Western Australia—Fiction.
Child sexual abuse by clergy—Western Australia—Fiction.

A823.4

A MEMORIAL TO WENDY,
AND A TRIBUTE TO LESLEY

ACKNOWLEDGEMENTS

I want to acknowledge my editor, Katia Ariel, and my publisher Catherine Lewis for the uncountable hours, the professional skill, the imagination and the tact they both devoted to turning my original draft into a publishable form. But even more than that I want to thank my wife Lesley, who has lived with this story over several years, reading numerous drafts, suggesting more modifications than I can remember, discussing the psychological plausibility of various turns of events, and above all encouraging me all the way.

AUTHOR'S NOTE

The characters and events in this story are not meant to represent any real people or events. Butler's *Lives of the Saints*, however, is a real book: a respected source of pious Catholic reading that has gone through numerous editions, revisions, additions and subtractions since its first publication in the 1750s.

While this book is a piece of fiction set largely in the 1950s, it resonates strongly with the present time and the deluge of revelations about sexual abuse of children, committed and protected within supposedly respectable institutions. Various organisations have been involved, but the Catholic Church has made a disproportionately generous contribution to the disgrace. Many must have been mystified about how an institution supposedly devoted to doing good has managed to harbour so much of the opposite. This story, as it follows a significant and ultimately transformative series of experiences in the life of a young man, provides a glimpse into aspects of the traditional culture of the church, shedding some light on a system that has stifled the spontaneous development of open sexuality, and fostered so much darkness.

John Watt
Busselton, Western Australia, 2015

1

Endings and Beginnings

He wakes again just before dawn. Reaches out for her again, almost feeling the comforting curves of her back and her hips, puzzled for a few seconds by her absence. And remembers. Turning onto his back and staring up at the emptiness of the ceiling, he searches his mind for something less bleak than this overwhelming sense of loss. He tries to distance himself from it, to think with more detachment about the strange tricks of memory: the way his mind at rest seems to pull a consoling blanket over the painful consciousness that, after all those years with her, he is finally alone, so that the awareness emerges to gnaw at him anew, even more painfully, each time he leaves the sanctuary of sleep.

He clambers out of bed, conscious of an awkward stiffness in his legs and a tight feeling at the back of his neck and across his shoulders. Surely that wasn't there ten or fifteen years ago. Is it realistic to think, at seventy-five, of getting back into better physical condition? Perhaps not.

What shape can his life take from this time on? He trawls his memory for a couple of lines that fit his situation rather well.

I have lived long enough. My way of life is fallen into the sere, the yellow leaf. Something like that. *Macbeth*, probably. He's not sure. It's a silly habit anyway, dredging up literary fragments to fit situations. And he can't blame it on forty years spent teaching English literature. He can remember doing it before he started teaching. The seed was probably planted at the seminary. Fragments from that course in English literature still leap out from his memory at times to surprise and move him.

The kitchen's a mess. He hasn't seen the point of washing up after every meal since his daughters and grandchildren did a major clean-up the day after the funeral and he stood out on the footpath the following morning watching them drive down the street and disappear around the corner. He looks around the bench tops and the sink, deciding today might have to be the day. After breakfast perhaps.

The funeral. It's odd that he remembers so little about it. He drifted through it surrounded by a mist. He has blurred images of several people standing, speaking, but very little recollection of what they said. Funerals are supposed to help the living to accept the finality of what has happened. Closure—that's the fashionable word—but it didn't seem to work for him. Once during the ceremony he even found himself turning to her to share a smile about something flattering that someone was saying about her, only to find, with a momentary shock, that of course she was not there. She was not anywhere. But it still didn't seem possible.

Older memories push into the foreground. Not those of a couple of weeks ago—images over fifty years old, but sharp and clear. Why does memory work so selectively?

The funeral of a priest—or rather, an ex-priest. Though as he recalls the rules, a priest was held to remain a priest regardless of what he had done or what disgrace loomed over his head. Just one of a multitude of technical details in that former life. It seems so long ago that the memories, in spite of being so clear, feel like someone else's—as if he is looking on from a short distance at scenes in which other people are involved.

He had some misgivings about that funeral, but went in spite of them. It was an awkward occasion with few people there, other clergy most of them, conspicuously avoiding saying anything real about the man they had come to bury. Full of silences and denials and careful detours around what everyone knew: what the man had done, who had exposed him, how he had died, what had driven him to take that way out. Nothing was openly acknowledged; instead, smooth platitudes about a life spent in God's service.

In spite of the circumstances, or perhaps because of them, the diocese had organised a quite impressive farewell. Thomas remembers sitting in a pew behind the rest of the small congregation, looking up at the stained-glass windows above the altar of the cathedral and the carving around the pulpit. The pure voices of the choir boys traced the rising and falling line, like a series of Gothic arches, that opens the Gregorian Requiem. Later in the service when a couple of speakers recounted stages in the life of the departed, and experiences shared with him, Thomas sat listening to the omissions and evasions, going back over his own crucial part in the affair; imagining the expression on that narrow face as Father Kevin had sat on a bollard on the Fremantle wharf after midnight, tying his ankles together with a few feet of baler twine to make sure, even though he was a non-swimmer. Trying to guess at the level of fear in the priest's mind as he must have stood at the edge of the wharf looking down at the black surface of the water, working up enough courage for the jump.

Sometimes Thomas was inclined to blame himself, but decided ultimately that although he couldn't avoid a sense of pity for the man, and a residual feeling of regret, even a trace of guilt, it had been, all things considered, the right thing to do. But it had not been well received—at least not in that company. He was right to have misgivings about the reception that awaited him where the usual groups formed under the trees at the entrance to the cemetery after the cathedral service, and as people drifted away from the graveside after the burial. It was impossible to exclude him from the occasion, but nobody spoke to him. He moved around trying without success to find a place where he could feel comfortable. Once he thought he overheard a fragment of conversation about how timely Father Kevin's departure was—now the unpleasant affair would not be dragged through the courts and the newspapers. Several times he thought he saw men, priests mostly, brother-priests of the man they were burying, as they would have put it, looking at him out of small groups, turning away when he met their eyes, shutting quiet conversations down as he passed. It was obvious then, though he had really known it already, that his actions had swept him decisively away from nearly everything and everybody that had moulded his life up to the events culminating in that funeral. He would have to find another shape for his life in another world. What that shape might be was far beyond his imagination.

She came into his life only a few months later, during his first year at the university, looking for a new direction, beginning to discover that the world was much wider and in some ways rather less wicked than he'd been led to believe. Though there's wickedness to be found everywhere.

Someone had introduced them—he can't recall who. It seems now, looking back, that the occasion marked the beginning of his real life, as if what came before was fantasy. She admitted much later that she'd had a speculative eye on him for some time and had engineered the meeting. He himself was totally inept and ignorant in negotiations of that sort; it was unexplored territory. Wilderness. He can still picture the setting quite clearly: the square of lawn, the fish pond, the façade of the university hall with its clock tower. And her.

'Thomas', she had repeated, looking rather dubious. Too formal for her. She'd call him Tom if he didn't mind. He remembers, with a smile. A beginning. There was a great deal more than his name that was destined to be reshaped. At first he was surprised by her directness, almost taken aback. In time he learned to appreciate it, to recognise it as a level of honesty that he hadn't encountered before. They had shaken hands on that occasion. It seemed to him at the time that their hands remained in contact rather longer than a casual introduction required. He recalls the strange combination of sensations he felt during that extended moment of contact: a sudden surge of excitement flooding his whole body, which he hoped was not as obvious as he feared it might be, combined with tightness in his belly, an insecure feeling that this moment might mark the opening-up of some unpredictable possibilities. As indeed it did.

The kitchen table is strewn with letters and cards of sympathy. Cards for her. No. Cards *about* her. He must do something about organising them as well as the dishes. Wonders what people usually do. Would all those well-wishers expect a response from him?

His mind retreats into the past, to a distant memory of another card. It was for her birthday, only a week before they married. He had written *With all my love forever*, having been feeling his way gradually into territory that he had not explored until the previous couple of years.

She kissed him, then pulled back a little and looked steadily into his eyes. He must not promise her all his love, she said. They will have children, and he must keep some love for them. And *forever* is too much to promise. *Till death do us part* is as much as anyone can sign up for. Nothing lasts forever. It was a long time before he had learned enough honesty from her to look at the facts of life with just a little of the same clear-sighted courage. He remembers her occasional sadness in her last years at the thought, which she expressed with the same honesty, that one of them was sure to go first and the other would be left alone.

He moves out to the back veranda. Ahead of sunrise the eastern sky is streaked with pale pink, repeated at closer range in a profusion of flowers on the massive apple blossom hibiscus against the back fence. It's the only plant he can remember choosing himself; the garden is usually her business. *Was* her business.

She had been puzzled over why he was so definite about wanting that variety when he usually had no views about plants of any sort. And there were so many new varieties; every old garden had an apple blossom hibiscus.

He found it difficult to explain that this was just the point. It stood in his mind for the ordinary world of backyards and back verandas and shared beds and shared lives and children and grandchildren and the normal varieties of innocent human pleasure. And pain. Anyway, there it still stands, grown tall and broad and flowering splendidly more than forty years later.

He wonders whether that other apple blossom hibiscus is still standing. It looked like an old shrub then, fifty years ago and more. Probably by now it's only a memory—an image that pulls back with it a chain of other memories about someone who now seems like a stranger: himself when young. He thinks of Omar Khayyam, a voice from nine hundred years past, speaking thoughts that could be his own. *Myself when young did eagerly frequent Doctor and saint, and heard great argument.*

Himself when young—now a stranger who seems to have lived in another world, seen at a great distance, as if on the far side of a huge expanse of water. But the memories from that distant time and place have remained clear, and now, against the new blankness of his present and his future, they stand out even more sharply.

He sits on one of the two old cane chairs on the veranda, unable to shut out the emptiness of the other chair beside him, remembering the day when he'd painted them, and called her out to see what a strange colour the paint had turned out to be: a peculiar purplish-pink. Not at all what he'd had in mind. It didn't matter, she said, that colour would do.

He tries to push his thoughts in a less painful direction, looking up into the beginning of the new day. Tries to pinpoint the time when the first fine cracks began to appear in the wall enclosing that remote world of the mind where he lived for his first twenty-three years. Perhaps the beginning of the end was that first consultation.

2

The Unravelling Begins

Thomas's neck feels sticky with sweat. He runs a finger around the inside of his collar. Uncomfortable things, clerical collars, especially in summer. Nine years in the seminary and he still doesn't feel at ease in one. Perhaps that's the point of them: daily mortification of the flesh.

He picks up a magazine. *Time*, a couple of months old. Skims an article on the American plan to test another nuclear bomb at Bikini Atoll. Possibly a series of them. A terrible weapon, as the archbishop had written in last week's issue of *The Catholic View*, but necessary for the free world to contain the spread of communism.

The phone on the receptionist's desk rings once, then stops, and she turns towards Thomas.

'Dr Macpherson is ready for you now.' She points to the door on the far side of the room.

He stands and crosses the room, very conscious of his legs. They seem to have impulses of their own, making jerky movements that are not fully under his control. He pushes the door open and steps stiffly into the next room.

A man with greying sandy hair looks up from a desk.

'Mr Riordan. Thomas Riordan, I understand. Shut the door, if you don't mind, and take a seat in this chair. And please excuse me for a minute or two while I finish a couple of notes.'

He goes back to jotting in a large notebook.

Thomas lowers himself cautiously into the chair. It's a bulky, low-seated, leather-covered piece of furniture, apparently designed without regard to the shape of the human body. He hesitates between sinking back out of control and perching upright on the edge, before finally choosing to perch.

He rubs the palms of his hands together nervously, feeling acutely aware of how conspicuously his knees are jutting up and out in front of him. He tries stretching his legs out straight with his heels on the floor. Now his substantial black shoes are standing up, toes pointing to the ceiling. This feels even clumsier. He pulls his feet back. The inconvenient knees jut up again.

Macpherson continues to write, and Thomas risks a quick direct look. Sees a middle-aged face, lean, and lined around the mouth and eyes, the greying hair cut fairly short. He thinks about the voice, the little that he heard of it. Perhaps there was a touch of Scots in the accent. The desk is bare except for the notebook in which its owner is still writing. What would he be writing about? About Thomas himself? And if so, what?

A window in the wall behind the desk looks out to an unkempt garden, overgrown shrubs merging together into a tangled dark-green barrier along the fence line.

Three walls of the room are lined with shelves almost to the ceiling, crammed with books. Substantial, serious books, most of them. He turns to focus on the shelf nearest to him.

David Hume, *Treatise of Human Nature*. Thomas Hobbes, *The Leviathan*. The names had been mentioned in lectures at the seminary. Philosophers, so-called. Sceptics, atheists, scoffers at religion. Dangerous authors. Their books are to be avoided. Benedictus de Spinoza, *Ethics*, another of the same. He has not read these books. Neither, he thought, had the lecturer who warned the students against them.

He turns back. The older man's eyes are on him. He's been watched—for how long? Perhaps the note-jotting was a screen from behind which he'd been watched for most of the time.

'Are you interested in philosophy, Mr Riordan? You have some of my favourites here. David Hume, now, a great thinker. An Edinburgh man, I believe, as I am myself, originally. Do you know his work?' His speech is controlled, tidy, like his desk.

Thomas hesitates, uncertain how much to admit.

'Not . . . not in much detail.'

'Ah, well. A pity. But we're not here to talk about philosophy. We should make a start. And you should start by telling me how I might be able to help you.'

Thomas has been rehearsing answers to this inevitable question for days, but now he stumbles over words, shies away from any real answer.

'I'm not . . . I thought that the archbishop had probably . . . or perhaps the archbishop's secretary——'

'Yes, yes. One of those gentlemen has been in touch. The second, if I remember rightly. And no doubt one of them will pay my fee in due course. It's a matter of some importance to us Scotsmen.'

He smiles, a slight, wry smile. For a moment his expression is lighter, warmer.

'But my professional business is with you. I need to hear from you. What is it that you and I are setting out to achieve? What is the knot that needs to be unravelled?'

Thomas rubs his hands together between his knees, immediately aware of what an embarrassing habit this is, and of how difficult his knees are.

'It's to do with my memory. I mean my memories.'

Macpherson leans back in his chair, looking at the wall somewhere above the younger man's head. His silence calls for more.

'I seem to have lost some of them. Of my memories. Lost a few days of my life. I have no idea what I was doing over a few days.'

'Yes. And these few days. When were they?'

'Only . . . not long ago. Less than three months. The beginning of December. It's so . . .'

Thomas's answer dries up for a moment. He looks away from the older man's face thinking, *he must be well aware of the facts. The whole State is well aware of them.* The story was all over the newspapers, emerging in fragments day by day through a couple of weeks until it was overtaken by the close approach of Christmas. A small passenger plane on a regular flight between Perth and Albany on the south coast, with a pilot and eight passengers on board, failed to arrive at its destination or to be seen or heard over several small towns along its usual route. The assumption was that it had strayed disastrously off course and disappeared, possibly into the ocean.

Then a few days later a single survivor walked into Windy Harbour, a tiny cluster of fishing shacks far to the west of the proper course: a young man, twenty-three years old, a student priest on the verge of ordination, on his way to a short placement as parish assistant in Albany. He is miraculously unhurt except for sunburn and blistered feet, neither of them the sort of injury associated with plane crashes.

Searchers took another two days to locate the crash site in isolated forest country near the coast—what was left of the plane, and what was left of its other occupants.

But one was unaccounted for: a young woman. Trackers found evidence that she too had survived the crash without major injury. Footprints around the site suggested that she was walking with a limp, but without really serious difficulty. Two sets of prints led from the area to the coast a couple of miles away. There were traces of the same tracks heading west along the coast, though tracking was difficult across sandy beaches, where most marks were washed out daily by waves and tide, alternating with bare rocky headlands.

These few facts were clear and widely known. Two people had survived the crash and started on the trek to safety. And only one, the young student priest, had arrived at the cluster of fishing shacks that was the only place of human habitation along a hundred miles of wild coast. And that one survivor could say nothing about what had happened to the other. Or *would* say nothing; some reporting had been ambiguous, sceptical.

Macpherson's questions and silences press Thomas to recount all of this. Then he leans forward, elbows on the desk.

'Well, then. That is what we know. More or less. What we don't know, because of this gap in your memories, is what happened between the crash and your arriving at Windy Harbour. And my task, as I understand it, is to help you to recover those memories, if possible. Is that your understanding of the situation?'

Thomas nods, looking away.

'There's one point I'd like you to clarify for me. I don't fully understand why it is so important for you to recover the memories. No doubt I've done numerous things myself that I don't remember. But I don't consult analysts to get all my memories back. I'm probably better off for forgetting some of them.'

He smiles briefly, the same wry smile, and sits back in his chair.

Thomas, perched uncomfortably on the edge of the chair, looks at the floor.

'I've been studying for ordination. I was . . . I mean I am to be ordained a priest. Quite soon.'

'So I gathered. A Roman Catholic priest.'

The young man considers the word *Roman* which is almost never used among Catholics about themselves. It's seen as verging on an insult. After all, what other sorts of Catholics are there? Should he take offence? Was it meant to be provocative, perhaps only slightly? Probably not. He picks up the thread of his explanation.

'The archbishop wanted things clarified . . . Before it would be appropriate to, or possible to——'

'Things clarified. I take it he meant what happened during the period that is missing from your memory. You will not be ordained until that is established. Is this the situation?'

Thomas nods.

'I surmised that much already. But I'm still not sure I fully understand why this is such an issue. Sending you to me—it seems a fairly extreme step with my not sharing your religious persuasion. Or any other persuasion either. In fact I don't think there's anyone in the state who shares both my profession and your religion. I wonder how that could be explained. But that's beside the point. Can you help me to a better understanding of why it is so important to recover these memories?'

Thomas rubs his hands together. How to explain this adequately, to a non-Catholic? Even a professed non-believer of any sort. He can't remember meeting anyone before who admitted to having no religion. He wonders how it is possible for anyone to make this admission so calmly. Casually. He looks at the floor under Macpherson's desk, fumbling for the right words.

'A Catholic priest. We are expected to be models of . . .'

He leaves the sentence hanging, unable to summon up an ending for it that will not create more problems. An image drifts up of Father Phelan, the rector, delivering his last homily to the final-year students at the seminary not long before the disaster. Fragments that stood out for him then come back to him now. *You are to be in the world, but not of the world. We are all born sinners; it is the ordinary human condition. But a young man worthy of the priesthood must strive to rise above the ordinary human condition. And must, at least to some very slight degree, succeed in rising above it. A priest who is a known sinner brings the whole of God's Church into disrepute. Saintliness. The struggle towards saintliness. It is the task you are called to. As I have been. No doubt none of us will achieve even a remote approach to it, but we must always strive, though always falling far short.*

The rector had stood facing the group for a good half minute in silence before leaving the lectern. Scanning them, his eyes pale behind their rimless glasses. Looking for something, as it seemed to Thomas; searching their faces, and whatever feelings or desires might hide behind them. The memory of those probing eyes brings back the familiar sense of general guilt, of unworthiness, the anxiety about having his short-comings exposed. His sins.

Thomas struggles for words, stumbles through the embarrassment of trying to make at least a little of this intelligible to an outsider. The word *sin* inevitably finds a place in his attempt, but he wonders how it will be understood.

After several minutes Macpherson cuts in.

'I think I am just beginning to see one side of the point a little more clearly. At least as well as I am likely to, from my perspective. Your archbishop is anxious to be sure that there is no chance of a—what should I say—an embarrassing revelation. He will not employ you if there is a danger of something coming out of this plane crash story that could damage the good name of his organisation.'

Thomas listens in silence, feeling a prickly discomfort at this way of identifying the problem. How could anyone talk so flatly about his being employed, as if a priestly vocation was on the same level as becoming a dentist or a plumber? How is it possible to think of God's Church as just another organisation, like a business? This is alien thinking. Disturbing.

His thoughts are interrupted.

'But that is looking at the situation only from the point of view of your archbishop, as if the main aim is to help him make a management decision. My professional focus must be on you, not on anyone else. What outcome can we expect from our consultations for you? I'm not asking you to answer, I'm just raising the question. What is the issue for you? I am strongly inclined to think that there is one. I expect it will emerge gradually. And it might, I suspect, look rather different from your archbishop's issue.

'Another thing. You mentioned sin a few moments ago. I must tell you that the word is not part of my vocabulary. My professional vocabulary, I mean. You need to understand my position, as I need to understand yours.'

Macpherson's focus shifts away to the bookshelves near Thomas's chair. He scans a shelf, his expression suddenly lighting up.

'Yes! There it is.' He leaps up with surprising vigour, darts across to the shelves, picks out a book, begins leafing through the pages. 'Another of my favourites: Spinoza. A wonderful philosopher. Have you read him?'

Thomas vacillates, replying cautiously, 'Only a little.' Then worries: does that amount to a lie, a sin, then? Not a mortal sin. Perhaps a venial sin. Probably. Certainly.

Macpherson thrusts the open book into his hands.

'Here it is. A marvellous passage. Just look at it.' He points to a short section, heavily underlined. The younger man focuses, realises with surprise that the book is in Latin. 'You read Latin, of course. I'm aware that it's the official language of your church. How would you translate that?'

Thomas is caught off balance. He is familiar with the Latin formulae of the liturgy, but this is something else altogether. He makes a tentative beginning.

'I have tried——'

The older man cuts in with a spontaneity and enthusiasm that he has not shown before. '*Sedule*. How would you put that into English? *Sedulously* won't do. What about *earnestly*? Or *conscientiously*?'

Thomas goes on, secretly glad of the prompt. 'I have tried conscientiously not to laugh, or to weep, or to lay blame, but to understand.'

'Just so. Isn't that wonderful? It should be the official motto of the psycho-analytic profession. And Spinoza our patron saint. If it ever became possible for a non-religious Jew to qualify as a saint. I suspect that he might not be an eligible candidate at present.'

Thomas catches a fleeting glimpse of the same slight smile.

'We are not in the business of blaming people, you see. So no mention of sin, as I said before. No laughing at what people do, or weeping over it. Just an effort to understand how people think and act. And why. And in particular to help them understand for themselves. So . . .'

Macpherson reclaims the book and replaces it on the shelf, returns to his chair, sits back, silent for a moment.

'I would expect to be able to do something about your problem. Probably. Given a little time. This immediate problem, at least.' He leans forward, bringing the fingertips of his hands together, his elbows resting on the desk in front of him. 'I imagine that your training has introduced you to some of the ideas of Freud, Sigmund Freud. Another non-religious Jew, as it happens.'

Thomas can't summon up a response. Freud. Another of the dangerous thinkers they were warned against at the seminary. Sceptic. Atheist. Materialist. He looks away from the doctor's face.

'No? Another pity. But it doesn't matter for our purposes. I work with the idea that there is a great deal in our minds that we're not aware of. We have thoughts, memories, that have been pushed out of consciousness. Back around a corner, so to speak, out of sight, out of mind. It's usually because they were shocking, or frightening. We can't comfortably think about them. So they're turned off. But they're still there, somewhere. And we can get them back into consciousness, if we can find the right switch to turn them on again. That's a way of putting it.

'I would assume, you see, that your lost memories are like that. Something happened that was extremely upsetting, and the memories around it have been pushed into the unconscious part of your mind. But people recover repressed memories much older than yours. Years. Even decades. Yours can be recovered. Almost certainly. If it is important to you to recover them.'

Thomas, listening, suddenly becomes aware of how tense his shoulders are and how tightly his fists are clenched. He goes back over Macpherson's last few words, wondering whether there was a trace of a suggestion that he might be hiding something deliberately.

'It's not that . . . I really can't remember. I try, all the time. But nothing comes.'

'No, no. You misunderstand. Most people do at first. I understand. You genuinely can't remember. Repression of memories isn't deliberate. It just happens. Remember this. No blame, no sin. These are not useful ideas.'

Macpherson sits back in his chair. 'Well, then. How are we going to proceed?' He is silent for a moment, looking up at the ceiling. He leans forward, his focus shifting down to Thomas's face.

'Tell me. When you arrived at that little fishing place . . . what's it called?

'Windy Harbour.'

'A splendid name, isn't it? What clothes were you wearing then? And were you carrying anything with you?'

'What clothes? I was wearing trousers and a shirt like these. But no jacket, or collar. And no shoes. And . . .' He falters, avoiding the older man's eyes. Remembering reports of the extended search by police and others along the coast. Various items of men's clothing found at locations east of Windy Harbour. Items of women's clothing also. The reports didn't specify what items of women's clothing they were. Speculation bloomed. But nothing emerged from the search except speculation. Thomas does not want to think about what some people might have imagined. Especially non-Catholics. There is a half-minute of silence.

'Ah, well. Apart from clothes. Were you carrying anything?'

Thomas seizes on the end of the difficult silence. 'Yes. A haversack, a rucksack. One of those hikers' rucksacks.'

'And inside it? What was inside?'

'Water bottles, some biscuits, a few nuts. That sort of thing.'

'I see. Just what you needed for a few days' trek along the coast. How did you come to have these things? Were they yours?'

Thomas shakes his head. 'Not mine, no. I only know what I read in the papers. Later. And they talked to me—the police,

I mean. Those things belonged to another passenger. He died in the crash. But how I came to be carrying them, I can't remember anything about that.'

'So. Was there anything else? Especially anything that belonged to you. Anything personal.'

'One thing, yes. I had a book.'

Thomas notices Macpherson sitting upright, eyes focusing on him more intently. 'A book. Now what book was that? A novel?'

The young man replies hesitantly. 'It was *Lives of the Saints*. Butler's *Lives of the Saints*. The abridged edition.' And wonders, while answering, why he is adding that extra detail.

'Ah.' Macpherson breathes out, a long breath. 'Butler's *Lives of the Saints*. I don't believe I've read it. This is interesting. The one thing out of your personal belongings that you salvaged and carried for, was it, four days? It must be important to you. Can you explain why?'

Thomas searches his mind for a way to begin. How to explain? A good Catholic would not need any explanation. Would certainly not ask for one.

'It's not easy to——'

Macpherson cuts in sharply on the pause. 'Try. Do your best to make me understand.'

He begins, hesitantly, searching for the words to make this intelligible. To show how this fits into the larger pattern of traditional piety. The general obligations required of everyone: Mass attendance, confession, Holy Communion, abstinence from meat on Friday. The more optional rituals: benediction, novenas, the rosary, and among the seriously devout, a range of individual practices of piety. Some profess a special attachment or devotion to one or other of the saints: pray for his or her help in difficult situations, make the corresponding saint's day a day of special celebration, and so on.

Early in his time at the seminary he came to understand that something of this sort was expected of him: a sign of the personal piety that should mark a young man called to the service of God. What he didn't understand was how he was to choose a private devotional practice like this. How did other people choose? How, also importantly, did they make their choices known? This was never explained.

Then for his birthday a present arrived from a pious aunt. A book: *Lives of the Saints*. Providential. His choice was made for him, and it was a distinctive choice. Other people might profess a personal devotion to one saint or another. His personal devotion would extend to the whole calendar of the saints. For every date, the book offered sketches of the lives of one or more saints. His practice would be to read every day about the life of one saint who is celebrated on that day, and to ponder on the lessons to be learned from the story. He would do this privately, but not so privately as to prevent his piety being noticed. It would be observed, probably without comment, but with approval. Even, perhaps, with admiration.

Thomas, eyes on the floor, struggling to explain at least some of this outside the circle within which it is already understood, feels himself to be stumbling through a swamp of embarrassment. His explanation begins to falter. He glances at the older man, finds eyes and attention fixed on him. Looks away again at the floor, past his knees that still jut awkwardly up and out in front of him.

'To you, I suppose, this must sound rather unusual.'

'No, no! Or rather, it doesn't matter a jot how unusual it might sound to me. It could be useful; that is the point. I expect it to be useful. You salvaged that book and carried it with you. Did you go on with the daily readings?'

'I don't know. I can't remember. Perhaps I did. Probably. I hope so.'

'Let's both hope so. Perhaps for different reasons. For me it provides a convenient way to proceed. A promising way. Possibly this book can provide the switch to turn your missing memories back on.

'We will need a series of consultations; it's impossible to predict how many. But before we make a real start I will need a better understanding of the background from which you come to me. Especially your personal history. You were born in Australia, I imagine.'

Thomas nods. 'Yes. Down in Albany.'

'And your parents, were they Australian-born too?'

'No, they were both born in Ireland. They came here from the Old Country as children. With their families.'

'They're both alive and well?'

'Yes they're still in Albany, running a grocery shop that they've owned for years.'

'What about brothers and sisters—do you have any?'

'Yes, there're three of us boys: I'm the second. But no sisters.'

'Now this family of yours—would you describe it as a particularly religious family?'

Thomas looks past Macpherson to the window, and hesitates before replying. He wonders what is the point of digging for all these family details? What connection could they have with his loss of memory? What is this man trying to get at? But a response is obviously expected.

'I suppose we're more religious than some. We always went to Mass every Sunday morning. Benediction often on a Sunday evening. Naturally we, the boys I mean, went to Catholic schools. We were all altar boys in the parish church. The parish priest would sometimes visit for a cup of tea. That sort of thing.'

Macpherson raises his eyes from the notebook in which he has been jotting.

'That's an interesting word to choose. *Naturally*. I don't suppose that going to Catholic schools happened literally as a natural result of anything. Wasn't it something your parents *chose*—to send you to Catholic schools?'

Again Thomas feels a faint unease; the question feels needlessly intrusive. What could hang on his answer?

Macpherson picks up on his hesitation. 'Perhaps some of these details seem irrelevant to you. But please trust me, they may turn out to be quite important. And not only for the project of reclaiming your memories.'

Thomas still hesitates momentarily, wondering what other project could be in question. But he attempts a response.

'I don't think they would have seen it as something to think about and decide. It was the only thing to do. Catholic parents send their children to Catholic schools. That is the way they would have seen it.'

The doctor rubs his chin with one hand, looking directly at Thomas with an expression that is hard to read—perhaps as if he is considering probing that last response, but deciding against it. He goes on, 'Your schools. Can you tell me a little about them?'

Thomas finds this an easier question to manage.

'I started at the local convent. Then I went on to the Brothers' school. The boys had to move to the Brothers' by the time they turned eight.'

'I see. So the nuns—I assume you were taught by nuns at the convent school—the nuns catered for boys and girls together, but only up to the age of seven. I wonder why it was thought that you needed to be separated so young. But we won't go into that just now. I am particularly interested in the institution where you have been training to be a priest. The seminary. I gather that you have graduated from it quite recently. If graduation is the appropriate word. How old were you when you started there?'

'I was fourteen. Just over fourteen. That was when I started at Saint Aloysius's here in Perth. The last four years I was over in Sydney at Saint Finian's.'

Thomas looks up to see the older man's eyes fixed on him. Macpherson puts down his pen.

'So you have been training to be a priest for—how long is it—nine years? You're twenty-three now.'

Thomas nods agreement.

'How did you come to start on this path? You must have been only thirteen when the plans were made. Who initiated them? That's a very early age for any decision like that. Was it what you wanted? Was the idea yours? Was it regarded as normal for boys to begin the training so young?'

Thomas runs a couple of fingers around the inside of his clerical collar. He is set back by this sudden flood of questions, and pauses, considering which of them to attempt first.

'The age, it's quite normal. Quite common. Some of us start earlier, some later.'

He contemplates the other questions. Whose idea had this been? Did he himself want this, make the decision? Not exactly. Of course that was an outsider's way of looking at it. It was not really a question of what he wanted to do: more one of what he was called to do. What God was calling him to do. That is the Catholic view of it. He may not want to at all. He may recoil from the idea. But is God calling? How many times did the rector address the students along these lines? Dozens, scores, certainly. Possibly even hundreds. How many stories has he heard and read, about saints who struggled for months or years against a divine calling, before finally accepting the will of God?

He thinks about his last year at the Brothers' school. He was thirteen. The word had been spread around his small world that he had all the signs of a vocation to the religious life, and would be going to the seminary the following year. He remembers the origin of this process, when he expressed some interest during one of the recurrent intensive drives at school to attract the students to a future as a priest or a brother. He remembers moments of panic over the year as he realised that the passing interest was being treated as a decision; the news was spreading and appropriate arrangements were being made. The teachers all knew, the family knew, the parish priest and his curate knew. The shape of his life was rapidly slipping out of his control, moving in a direction that he had not anticipated. How much of this should he try to explain to this man? He can imagine how it might be understood, perhaps rather misunderstood, by someone outside the circle of faith. And not without reason, he can see that. But if, as has been stressed so often, the controlling hand was the hand of God, what was he to do?

Macpherson is speaking again.

'The seminary, or I should say the seminaries, as you have attended two of them: are they residential institutions? I'm interested in understanding how much of your life they have occupied over the last nine years, and how much of your time you spent elsewhere. Living with your family, for instance.'

Thomas feels more comfortable; this seems safer territory.

'Yes, we lived in at the seminary. At Saint Aloysius's we went home for the usual school holidays. We could have visitors there every second Sunday afternoon, and some of us had regular visits. But my family was in Albany running the shop, which kept them busy down there. When I was in Sydney I got home once a year at Christmas. And the programmes took up most of our time; we didn't go out from either place much at all.'

The older man jots a few words in his notebook, and then looks up again.

'I see. So from what you tell me it seems that you haven't lived in a family situation or had a great deal of family contact since you were, I think you said, just fourteen.' He pauses, looking up at the ceiling for a few moments before going on. 'I had supposed something like that would be the situation, but what you describe, it goes beyond what I had imagined.'

He pauses again, looking at the wall somewhere above Thomas's head, then focuses back on him.

'I want to explore another approach that might be fruitful. Tell me, Mr Riordan, do you often have dreams that you remember after you wake?'

Thomas wonders about the sudden change of direction.

'Yes, I dream sometimes. I don't know how often—or how often other people dream. It's not something we talk about much, the people I know.'

'A pity perhaps. There's a lot to be learned from our dreams. And from thinking about them. This is what I want you to do. When you wake up from a dream, especially a vivid one, spend a few minutes going over the details. Try to fix them in your memory. Perhaps make a few notes about it. The next time we meet I will ask you to tell me about it. It may help us to unravel a few issues.

'I have already pencilled in the same time next Friday for our second meeting. Apart from any dream you might have had, please bring the book with you, *Lives of the Saints.* And resist the temptation to look back at the stories for those days that have dropped out of your memory. Until next week.' The faint smile lightens his face again. 'I imagine that resisting temptation is a habit that you have cultivated more conscientiously than most of us.'

Thomas listens, uncertain about how to react. Is Macpherson laughing at him? Or laughing at himself? Has the consultation finished?

'One question, Mr Riordan, before you go. It has nothing to do with our professional relationship; it's just to satisfy my curiosity.'

The younger man, hands on the arms of the chair ready to hoist himself upright, settles down again.

'The Latin language. I had to learn a little of it myself. Heaven knows why it was supposed to be part of a proper old-fashioned schooling. As far as I knew it hadn't been in ordinary use for centuries. But it's still used in the services of the Roman Catholic Church.'

Thomas agrees, registering again the word *Roman*. Wondering again whether it is intended to be slightly provocative. He is unsure. Perhaps not. Probably not.

'I've never attended one of your regular services, but I understand that they are conducted almost entirely in that language. I have been to two or three funerals in churches of your persuasion. Perhaps more. Weddings too. Even one christening. Because of connections with relatives and friends. I was surprised to hear Latin even on more personal occasions like those. As far as I could judge most of the congregation showed no sign of understanding much of it. Would you say this was fairly typical?'

Thomas considers. Is it typical? He thinks of the congregation in Saint Brigid's last Sunday. The shuffling, the coughing, the crying babies, the restless children, the elderly nodding off in the pews. Father Kevin rattling through the ritual at high speed. With some reluctance he agrees, wondering what congregations are like in non-Catholic churches.

Macpherson nods. 'I was puzzled at the time about the point of conducting services in a language that most of the people didn't understand. Can you explain this for me?'

Thomas hesitates. The reasons for the use of Latin. Children in Catholic schools are taught the reasons. He rehearses them in the back of his mind. He is not sure how they would sound to a non-Catholic. Should he try to explain his feeling about this from a priest's point of view? A certain feeling about being initiated, step by step, into an inner group, with its own special power and knowledge, a magic of its own, framed in its own language, inaccessible even to most of the Catholic laity. Further still, beyond the comprehension of the world at large.

How would this be understood by someone far outside the circle of faith? He is unsure, insecure about exposing himself so far. He answers cautiously, tentatively.

'I suppose it's mainly just traditional.'

The doctor listens, considers, feeling the weight of the answer. He looks dubious.

'Traditional. I suppose that is a reason. One sort of reason.' He pushes back his chair and stands. 'Well then. We shall see each other at the same time next Friday. And you will bring the book. You may also have a dream to tell me about.'

3

A Pastoral Visit

Thomas turns the corner. In front of him is the last stretch of the twenty-minute walk from the bus stop to Saint Brigid's Parish Presbytery. Is it home? Home has been a difficult idea for him. For years he has been unable to think of the family home as anything but a place to spend holidays. He has eaten, slept, studied, and prayed in two seminaries, but it has been just as difficult to think of either of those cold places as a real home. Now the presbytery has to be home of a sort, perhaps, for the time being. A trial posting as parish assistant, the archbishop had said, just until the issue of his ordination was ... clarified. He had paused, hesitated, looking out of the window at the old palm trees in the garden before settling on the right word. Thomas had noticed how plump and smooth his face is. And his hands.

He hates this last stretch. An unkerbed roadway with the bitumen edges breaking up, and an uneven footpath of pale grey concrete slabs, most of them cracked and broken. Between the path and the road there is a strip of road verge, dry and sandy, with a few thin stands of dead wild oats bleached pale at the end of the long dry summer. Outside two or three of the houses the verge shows a patchy green, with token fences of small sticks and string to keep the neighbours' cars and children and dogs off the struggling grass. The defences have not worked well against the dogs.

It's a modest street in a very modest suburb full of small houses with walls of fibro sheet or home-made cement brick. He passes a few of them, waiting for their owners to find the time and the money to finish a side sleepout or a front veranda.

Thomas measures his progress towards the parish buildings at the far end. Every twenty-two paces, with due allowance for side streets, there is or ought to be a tree. Since the corner he has counted eleven clearly alive, five clearly dead, three apparently undecided, and seven spaces where the attempts to improve the street have disappeared altogether, probably to improve some of the local backyards. It will be a long wait before the survivors do much to soften the scene; the best of them are no taller than Thomas himself.

He thinks about Macpherson's suggestion that there might be two problems to be explored in their consultations, the task of recovering lost memories being only the more obvious one. He finds this suggestion puzzling, and a little unsettling. The doctor distinguished the archbishop's concern from a possible issue that related more directly to Thomas himself, but he does not see what this might be.

At the front of one of the houses a young woman is holding a hose, watering a tiny square of garden. There are small plants around the edge with orange flowers that look to be a little past their prime. He searches his memory for a name, and the word *calendula* appears. Possibly that's the right word.

His grandfather would have known. In the centre of the bed is one rose bush, with a couple of pink buds beginning to open.

The woman turns now and then to spray the feet of a little boy, who squeals and pretends to run away, then dashes behind his mother to wait for another staged surprise. She pretends ostentatiously to have lost him, calling and looking in every direction except behind, while he stifles giggles and catches Thomas's eye. Thomas slows his stride, then stops for a few moments to watch the game.

His attention is caught by her movements: the way the curves of her hips and thighs shape the skirt of her dress as she swings the hose around. He finds himself imagining what she might be wearing under her dress—and what she would look like under that layer. He notices her neckline, lower than he is accustomed to seeing outside the church on a Sunday morning. The curves of her breasts and the cleavage between them are plain to see. Excitement flares up like a flame.

She swings around with the hose again. Her eyes meet his, and quickly scan him up and down, with a startled expression. One hand moves up defensively to the top button of her dress. The hose drops, and she hurries to the tap to turn it off, picks up the little boy and talks to him as she turns towards her front door, asking what he would like to have for tea when daddy comes home.

Thomas looks away, embarrassed. She seemed alarmed. Did she think he was staring at her? Did she see the signs of arousal in his trousers? But he couldn't help being aware of the curves of her breasts behind the thin summer dress. There's no sin in that, in just noticing. No, it was not just noticing; he had been focusing, continuing to focus, losing control of his eyes, and then his thoughts. There is sin here.

He heads off along the uneven, cracked footpath. His legs move jerkily; they feel beyond his control. The soles of his substantial black shoes make clomping noises on the path. The edge of a badly broken paving slab catches one shoe, and he stumbles, but manages to recover awkwardly, hoping that she is not watching his ineptitude. He wonders why clumsiness often overcomes him in situations like this.

He hears the front door of the little house slam shut behind the woman, and looks back. It's a bright red door, a nice touch to liven up the drab fibro home. He wonders what it would be like to be part of that family group. Imagines himself coming home from work (what sort of work would he be doing?) to that house with its red door, and that little boy, and that woman with her thin summer dress and her breasts behind the dress, and her . . . Beyond breasts his imagination falters. He has only the vaguest idea of what to visualise. There is the inevitable onset of guilt about the direction his imagination is taking him, the physical arousal that he is unable to subdue. He looks ahead, trying to guess the distance left, trying to shut out the fantasy.

Thomas forces his attention in a more innocent direction. Tries to focus on a remembered image of his grandfather's garden at the side of the old house in the country town—an image from an island of memory that stands up steeply out of the surrounding sea. Memories about several months spent with his grandparents in a place of trees and wild rabbits and rampant blackberries and heat and dusty gravel roads. He tries to hold the image of the garden in view: the summerhouse, the monkey puzzle tree, the row of low plants in flower. Snapdragons. Recalling his five-year-old pleasure at opening their dragon mouths and seeing how neatly they snapped shut.

The image is suddenly overwhelmed by another, a memory from a later and more disturbing phase in his growing-up: fourteen or fifteen years of age. He is swimming in the river adjoining the seminary, looking up at a girl passing over the bridge on a bike. She is about the same age as him, and wearing an unfamiliar school uniform, so not from a Catholic school. Her black-stockinged legs push the pedals around rhythmically, allowing him glimpses of her pale thighs above her school stockings. He stares up, craning for more glimpses, hoping that he is out of sight and that the uncontrollable response of his body is hidden by the murkiness of the slightly muddy river water. Momentarily she turns her head, seems to focus on him peering up at her. As he turns away, worried about losing control again of his eyes and his imagination, she begins to pedal harder, hurrying to put more distance between them.

The approach to the church buildings calls his attention back from the past. Thomas passes the convent, then the convent school, and turns in at the church gateway. It's not an impressive building, the Walter Park church, with walls of grey concrete blocks and roof of grey corrugated asbestos sheet. Saint Brigid's. Dedicated to Ireland's favourite among the female saints. A great nation for saints, the Irish. It has high, narrow window openings, a gesture towards traditional would-be-Gothic church architecture. Half of them are filled with plain glass. The rest are covered with panels of used plywood peppered with nail-holes; even plain glass is expensive. There is a parish fund for real church windows, with stained-glass that will spread brilliant light onto the congregation on Sunday mornings through saints glowing in blue and red and gold. But the window fund has made almost no progress, and there is still a big debt owing on the building itself.

This is a poor substitute for the churches they built in the ages of faith. Thomas remembers a photograph from one of the few books in the seminary library, *Great Cathedrals of Europe*, of the façade of Chartres, he thinks. Carved stone, pale golden, with spires and gargoyles and niches for statues. Stained-glass windows framed in stone shaped as delicately as lace. Saints looking out from every recess and every window. If he half-closes his eyes he can almost see it, the real church, shining out from behind this mean grey barn. He can almost hear the music too, ancient singing to match the ancient building of his imagination. The splendid, solemn Gregorian music for Holy Week, leading to Good Friday. The Office of *Tenebrae*. Darkness. Gregorian music seems to suit shadow better than light. He feels part of an ancient tradition that will last forever, walled off from the passing fads and fashions of the outside world.

Father Kevin comes bursting out of the front door of the presbytery on the far side of the church.

'There you are, m'boy.' He fiddles with the stud at the back of his clerical collar. 'About time too. I was on the point of giving you up for lost and heading off by myself.' He shrugs the shiny black jacket straight on his skinny shoulders. It's still not quite straight. 'A treat for you. Take you out of yourself. Afternoon tea with Mrs Regan. I don't think you've met her yet. We'll walk. It's only a couple of blocks, and the Austin's low on petrol. Pray God nobody takes it into his head to die tonight. If we go out in the car we probably won't get home in it.'

Home. Father Kevin doesn't seem to hesitate about using the word.

The older man leads the way along the street and around the first corner. Thomas follows half a pace behind. He notices the small priest smooth the few remaining strands across the top of his shining bald head. The narrow face turns suddenly.

'And how did you get on with the witch-doctor? All your problems solved in one blow?' He grins with one side of his mouth.

Thomas shakes his head, spreading his hands out, feeling the awkwardness of the gesture.

'I don't think it's supposed to be like that. In one blow, I mean.'

Father Kevin snorts. 'Not surprising. Stands to reason. This new archbishop, I can't follow his reasoning sometimes. New-fangled ideas. In the old days a good retreat was enough to straighten anybody out. Starting with a solid dose of fire and brimstone. Clears out the system wonderfully. As good as castor oil any day.

'Mrs Regan now, she'll do you a power of good. To meet her, I mean. One of the old sort. Hard to find them these days, in this country anyway. Nine or ten children, good Catholics every one. Well, the youngest is only two or three years old. But he's sure to turn out a good Catholic. It's in the blood—pure Irish breeding. The father's a barman down at the Shamrock.'

They arrive at a timber house with remnants of dark green paint peeling off the weatherboards. The priest smooths the few hairs across the crown of his head again, and knocks.

The door is opened almost instantly by a thin woman with greying hair pulled back from a sallow face. There are worry lines around her mouth and her eyes. Thomas wonders if she was waiting anxiously in the passage for the knock.

She smiles nervously and bobs a little. 'Father Kevin, it's good of you to——'

'No, no Mrs Regan. It's good of you to invite us. I was just telling Mr Riordan here—but I'm neglecting my social obligations. Mrs Regan, Mr Riordan, Mr Thomas Riordan, my new parish assistant.'

Thomas notices a rounder and more fulsome tone in the older man's voice. He considers offering his hand, wonders whether that would be appropriate, but decides against it after some hesitation. The woman bobs again and looks modestly at the doorstep.

'Should I call you Father?'

Father Kevin answers for him.

'Not just yet, Mrs Regan. Mr Riordan is waiting for ordination. But it won't be a long wait, God willing. I was just telling him about your wonderful Catholic family. There aren't many like you around these days, more's the pity'.

He turns to Thomas with an unctuous smile. 'Now here's something I've often noticed, Mr Riordan. A woman who's used to cooking for a good big family, she can always find a morsel for the priest if he happens to call at a mealtime. Happy to do it. Generous. Plenty for another mouth. Not like those selfish little families that people are having these days. Only one or two children. Catholics too. At least, they call themselves Catholics.' He shakes his head. His voice has taken on a doleful tone. 'More money than heart. Only enough in the pot for themselves.' He shakes his head again, then brightens up visibly and audibly. 'But Mrs Regan, here, she's one of the old sort.'

There is another anxious smile from Mrs Regan.

'If you would like to come into the front room, Father, and Mr Riordan.' She points the way and stands aside for them, smoothing her apron down. Passing her, Thomas sees her at closer range; without the nervous smile she looks tired, even more lined. Not surprisingly, he thinks, trying to imagine the burden of feeding and clothing and managing nine or ten children.

Inside the front room the curtains are open only a few inches, and he peers into the dimness. There's enough light to see a room with some very familiar features. On one wall a large picture of Our Lady clothed in white and blue, treading the evil serpent underfoot, her head modestly covered by a nun-like veil, but crowned with shining stars. Over the mantelpiece, an even bigger picture. A couple of guardian angels, their feathered wings well displayed, are guiding two children away from some danger that is hard to identify; it might be a pool of water or a deep hole. A charming picture expressing a charming thought: every child watched over by its own guardian angel. Not exactly part of the creed, but a well-established pious tradition. Especially in Ireland.

In an instant Thomas's mind jumps to a story from one of the newspapers a few weeks earlier. A mother was helping a little girl down the steep steps of a bus. The door suddenly snapped shut trapping the toddler by one foot. The bus pulled out from the kerb and down the street, the little girl's head and shoulders bumping and dragging on the roadway, her mother running, shouting, screaming, the driver totally unaware.

By the time he was stopped the child had been gradually battered to death. What was her guardian angel doing? Even more shockingly, what was God doing?

Thomas shakes his head in an effort to dislodge the terrible images and the threatening questions. Especially that last frightening question. What is happening to him, that he can be doubting God's mercy? Where do they come from, these confronting ideas that seem to burst into his mind uninvited? Could this invasion of disturbing thoughts be a temptation from the devil? More than he can remember at any past time, he seems at present to be beset by temptations to sin, in the body and in the mind. There must be an answer to every question, but only God knows all, he reminds himself.

He looks further round the room. On a sideboard backed by a mirror stands a statue of the Sacred Heart. A big statue, for a small room cluttered with so much drab brown furniture. The holy face, on a level with his own, looks out at the world calmly, benevolently, but with a hint of reproach. One finger points significantly to the exposed bright red heart, with huge red drops of plaster blood caught in a frozen moment of dripping down towards the floor. The reflection in the mirror of the same figure from behind creates in Thomas a feeling of vague unease, a faint sense of generalised guilt.

Mrs Regan bustles past him. 'Would you like to sit here Father, and you over there Mr Riordan? I've baked some scones. With home-made jam. Fig jam. I hope you like them.' Her hands are clasped together and she peers from one to the other anxiously.

'Ah,' says Father Kevin. 'Scones. The good Sisters try occasionally but they never seem to get them quite right.

There's always something a little dry about them. Where would we be, Mr Riordan, without our Catholic family women? Good Catholic wives and mothers.'

He settles himself into what is obviously the best chair, with his hands on his belly. It is, Thomas observes, a surprisingly well-rounded belly, considering how scrawny he is in other quarters, and wonders why he has not noticed this before.

Mrs Regan, settled in her own chair, is looking a little less anxious.

'Maureen!' she calls. A shrill, penetrating call. 'Maureen! We're ready now.'

An extended period of clattering begins, originating at the rear of the house. Father Kevin's hands remain at rest across his belly. The Sacred Heart statue, finger pointing to the red plaster heart and the huge drops of bright plaster blood, and backed by its own rear-view reflection lurking in the mirror, gazes across the room from the vantage point of the sideboard. Under this faintly accusing gaze Thomas feels increasingly uncomfortable. Mrs Regan's hands fidget in her lap. She reaches up with one hand to get an errant strand of hair under control. Her worn, anxious expression is coming back. The clattering continues.

'Maureen! What in the name of God and his holy mother are you doing out there?'

Finally a tray appears in the doorway, with the promised scones and jam, and even whipped cream. It is carried by a nervous-looking girl, a younger, scrawnier and even more worried version of her mother.

'This is Maureen. You know her of course, Father. She's the second of the five, Mr Riordan. The five girls, that is. Just turned fifteen. She wasn't doing at all well at the convent.

Not like Mary, my first. She's the smart one, always top of her class in Religious Knowledge. We're hoping and praying that she'll enter when she finishes school. Enter the convent, that is. But Maureen . . .' She shakes her head. 'So I'm keeping her at home to help with the house. And the little ones.'

The girl is still standing in the middle of the room holding the tray and grinning nervously at the floor. Her mother shakes her head again.

'Well girl, put the tray down. The Fathers can't wait for ever. I mean Father and Mr Riordan. And where's the teapot? And the milk jug? And the hot water?'

The tray lands with a clatter on the low table. Maureen looks around for the missing items. There is a touch of desperation in her expression.

'I must have put them somewhere. I'll get them.' She scuttles out and reappears with another tray carrying the rest of the necessities.

'Thank you, Maureen. That will do very nicely. Now just run out to the back and see what Brigid is doing to little Brendan.' It's only then that Thomas becomes fully aware of the distant howling, and realises that it has been going on for some time.

The girl retreats, looking relieved. Mrs Regan sets about the important task of pouring tea. The sound of a couple of vigorous slaps comes down the passage from the back of the house, and the howling of little Brendan is reinforced by the howling of slightly bigger Brigid in a different key.

Father Kevin selects a scone with great care, splits it, and piles the halves with jam and cream.

'Well, now.' He sits back, admiring the result of his labours. His small eyes gleam. 'This is very pleasant.'

Mrs Regan looks over her shoulder at the Sacred Heart, then lowers her eyes piously.

'Perhaps, Father, you would like to say grace.'

Thomas too lowers his eyes. He waits. There is no response for some time. He looks up to see Father Kevin's mouth fully occupied by a large part of his first scone. The priest's narrow cheeks bulge. He chews vigorously, eyes watering from the effort of trying to clear a way for speech. Crumbs fall down the front of his shiny black jacket, and there is cream at the corners of his mouth. There is a loud gulp.

Finally he is able to utter a recognisable word.

'I think——' He swallows loudly again. His tongue darts out to salvage the cream around his mouth. 'I'm sure that Our Lord will take that as read. Or as said, I should say. In such a good Catholic home.' His eyes crinkle up in an expression of benevolent good humour, as he reaches for another scone and splits it, shuffling the halves around on the plate to find convenient spaces for them along with the substantial remains of the first, piling on more jam and cream.

He looks up, his mouth busy with another generous portion of scone, eyes settling on the statue.

'Now that,' he pauses to gulp down the mouthful, 'That is a very fine statue. Would I be right in supposing, Mrs Regan, that that statue came from the old country?'

Mrs Regan blushes with visible pleasure. Her hands flutter.

'That's right Father. It's a present from my old aunt in Galway. She won a little something on the horses. But how did you know it was Irish?'

Father Kevin bites into another scone and chews reflectively. A large bulge moves around one cheek. He looks the statue over.

'There's something about it. Maybe the colours. I often think that the copies they make in this country are not quite right. Not bright enough to be a really good likeness. This one is the genuine article.' His hand darts out for another scone. 'These scones,' he digs into the jam, 'and the jam too. The best I've ever had the pleasure of tasting, thanks be to God.' He reaches out for the cream.

Thomas watches Mrs Regan's face crease with pleasure. The small man turns towards him.

'But what about you, Mr Riordan? You're still toying with the first of Mrs Regan's magnificent scones. I'm sure she expects better than that from a healthy young seminarian.' He turns back and beams genially at the woman.

Thomas shakes his head. 'They're very nice. But I'm not especially hungry.'

Father Kevin raises his hands towards the ceiling and declaims something about the younger generation not being the men their elders were.

The front door opens, then slams shut, and a slightly built boy dressed in rumpled shirt and shorts appears momentarily, heading down the passage to the back of the house. Mrs Regan smiles.

'That's my boy, Michael, Mr Riordan. We're so proud of him. The youngest altar boy in the parish. Only just nine years old, and he spouts the Latin like a cardinal.'

The priest nods. 'I believe he's the youngest altar boy I've ever had. Wonderful. A real sense of reverence. It's an inspiration to see that lad at the altar with his hands joined and his eyes closed in prayer. It would not surprise me, Mrs Regan, if you had a future priest there. You might keep it in mind. In three or four years he'll be old enough to be sent to the seminary. It's not wise to leave it too long. Many a fine young lad has been distracted by the things of this world and lost a clear calling.'

Mrs Regan's skinny face glows.

'Do you really think so, Father?'

'I do indeed. The indications are all there. But of course these things are in God's hands.' He raises his eyes to the ceiling, then lowers them to the more earthly level of the table to survey what is left of the afternoon tea provisions. Thomas follows his glance. There are two scones left, but very little jam, and no cream at all.

The older man changes tack and tone.

'Well, Mr Riordan. I think it's high time we left Mrs Regan to the joys of her family life.' He stands briskly and heads for the passage and the front door, with Mrs Regan scurrying in his wake and Thomas bringing up the rear.

Thanks and farewells waste little time. Thomas notices the worn expression returning to the woman's face as she turns back into the house, and hears, or thinks he hears, a sigh. And wonders. Did she hope to have more of those scones left? Did she keep some of that cream aside? Is there any jam left in the jar? Do all those children enjoy whipped cream, or is it only for the priest? And what about Mrs Regan herself? He can't remember seeing her with a scone on her own plate. He wonders whether the priest has noticed the tired lines on her face and the paint peeling off the door frame. He notices and avoids a cracked floorboard as he steps down from the porch.

Outside and well clear of the house, Father Kevin turns, with a sly grin.

'There you are, m'boy. A useful lesson for you. It'll stand you in good stead when you have a parish of your own. Work out which of the women bake a good scone. Cultivate them. You should score at least one afternoon tea invitation a week from one or other of them, in my experience. On average. What I said about nuns, it's as true as I'm standing here. There's not a nun alive that can serve up a half-decent scone. Sometimes I think they deliberately leave them out in the weather for a day or two to toughen them up. Mortification of the flesh. I wish they'd stick to mortifying their own flesh, and treat mine a bit more gently. I tell you, m'boy, there's a devil of a lot more a parish priest needs to know, over and above what they teach you at the seminary.'

4

The Feast of Saint Sabas

Thomas sits stiffly upright, perching on the edge of the bulky, leather-covered chair. His legs are thrust straight out in front of him, knees tight together. His copy of *Lives of the Saints* rests symmetrically across them. He glances up. Macpherson is looking him over with the faintest of smiles.

'Well, now. Your first task is to relax. To begin with, sit back in your chair. That's better. Now let your arms and legs lose their tension. That's a great deal better. But look at your hands.'

Thomas looks down. His hands are clenched into tight fists; he had no awareness of it. He loosens his fingers.

'That's better still. Now close your eyes. Sit like that for a couple of minutes. Think of nothing. Or better, imagine yourself sitting in a bare room. No furniture, no doors, no windows, no pictures, no people. Just plain white walls and ceiling and floor.'

He sneaks his eyes open to a slit. Macpherson is jotting in his notebook. What could he be writing? He closes his eyes again, to see whiteness. It seems to be a long time.

'That's fine—you seem much more relaxed. Open your eyes now, and pick up your book.'

Thomas hoists himself forward onto the edge of his chair.

'No, no. Sit back again. Take another minute or so to be properly relaxed again. Now the book. I think you said that it's organised according to the calendar. What was the first day that seems to be missing from your memories?'

'The beginning of December. The first. I forget what day of the week.'

'Perhaps the day of the week is not important. Open the book at the first of December and we shall see what comes to light. If anything.'

Thomas leafs through the pages. 'Here it is, 1st December. The feast of Saint Sabas, abbot, 532 AD. That would be the year of his death.'

'Saint Sabas. Well, now, I don't believe I've ever heard of him. 532 A.D.; that's a longish time ago. No doubt I shall find this very informative. This is what I want you to do. Read the story of the life of Saint Sabas. Read it aloud. Sit back and relax while you are reading. But try to be alert for any images or thoughts that come to mind from the last time you read this story. Anything. Any memories that emerge: where you were, what you saw, or heard, or felt or smelled. Don't worry if it seems trivial. It might be only an itch on your ankle or a mosquito buzzing in your ear. Anything at all. When you finish the story you can tell me about whatever has floated to the surface.'

Macpherson sits back in his chair. Thomas begins.

Saint Sabas, one of the most renowned patriarchs of the monks of Palestine, was born at Mutalasca, in Cappadocia, not far from

Caesarea, the capital, in 439 [A.D.]. The name of his father was John, that of his mother, Sophia, both were pious, and of illustrious families. The father was an officer in the army, and being obliged to go to Alexandria, in Egypt, took his wife with him, and recommended his son Sabas, with the care of his estate, to Hermias, the brother of his wife. This uncle's wife used the child so harshly that, three years after, he went to an uncle, Gregory, brother to his father, hoping there to live in peace.

Gregory having the care of the child, demanded also the administration of his estate, whence great lawsuits and animosities arose between the two uncles. Sabas, who was of a mild disposition, took great offence at these discords about so contemptible a thing as earthly riches, and, the grace of God working powerfully in his heart, he resolved to renounce for ever what was a source of so great evil among men. He retired to a monastery, called Flavinia, three miles from Mutalasca, and the abbot received him with open arms, and took great care to see him instructed in the science of the saints, and in the rules of a monastic profession.

His uncles, blinded by avarice and mutual animosity, were some years without opening their eyes; but at last, ashamed of their conduct towards a nephew, they agreed to take him out of his monastery, restore him to his estate, and persuade him to marry. In vain they applied all means to gain their point. Sabas had tasted the bitterness of the world, and the sweetness of the yoke of Christ, and his heart was so united to God, that nothing could draw him from his good purpose.

He applied himself with great fervour to the practice of all virtues, especially humility, mortification and prayer, as the means to attain all others. One day, whilst he was working in the garden, he saw a tree loaded with fair and beautiful apples, and gathered

one with an intention to eat it. But reflecting that this was a temp-
tation of the devil, he threw the apple on the ground, and trod upon
it. Moreover, to punish himself, and more perfectly to overcome the
enemy, he made a vow never to eat any apples as long as he lived.

Thomas pauses, glancing up from the page. Macpherson, apparently jotting a comment in his notebook with a puzzled expression about his eyes, notices the pause and the glance.

'Now don't attend to me. I'm listening, never fear. Just focus on the story. And on whatever it brings back to you.'

Thomas goes on.

By this victory over himself he made great progress in all other
virtues, exercising himself by day in labour, accompanied by prayer,
and by night in watching in devotions, always fleeing idleness as
the root of all evils, sleeping only as much as was absolutely neces-
sary to support nature, and never interrupting his labours but to
lift up his hands to God.

When Sabas had been ten years in this monastery, being eighteen
years old, with the leave of his abbot, he went to Jerusalem to visit
the holy places, and to edify himself by the examples of the eminent
solitaries of that country. He passed the winter in the monastery of
Passarion, governed at that time by the holy abbot Elpidius. All the
brethren were charmed with his virtue, and desired earnestly that
he should fix his abode among them; but his great love of silence
and retirement made him prefer the manner of life practised by
Saint Euthymius. He cast himself at the feet of that holy abbot,
conjuring him with many tears to receive him among his disciples.

When he was thirty years of age he obtained leave of Saint
Euthymius to spend five days a-week in a remote cave, which time

he passed, without eating anything, in prayer and manual labour. He left his monastery on Sunday evening, carrying with him palm-twigs, and came back on Saturday morning with fifty baskets which he had made, imposing upon himself a task of ten a-day. Thus he had lived five years, till Saint Euthymius chose him and one Domitian for his companions in his great yearly retreat in the deserts of Rouban, in which Christ is said to have performed his forty days' fast.

They entered the solitude together on the 14th January, and returned to their monastery on Palm Sunday. In the first retreat Sabas fell down in the wilderness, almost dead from thirst. Saint Euthymius, moved by compassion, addressed a prayer to Christ, that he would take pity on his young fervent soldier, and, striking his staff into the earth, a spring gushed forth; of which Sabas, drinking a little, recovered his strength so as to be enabled to bear the fatigues of his retreat.

Macpherson intervenes.

'No doubt there is more, but we might leave the story here.'

Thomas closes the book and lays it on the bulky leather-covered armrest of the chair. The doctor leans forward, elbows on the desk.

'That's fine. Now close your eyes and relax. You read that story only a few weeks ago. Think yourself back into that time, that place. You put the story of Saint Sabas down, and you look around. What do you see? What do you feel, or hear, or smell?'

Thomas sinks back in his chair. He feels the smooth leather surface of the chair-back. And remembers. There is something different against his back: something massive and rough.

An enormous tree trunk. Behind closed eyelids he looks around. Trees are all around him: giants of a size he has never imagined. Sitting on the ground with his back against one of them, he looks up the trunk of another directly in front of him. It has a few feet of rough bark near the ground, and above that it is smooth and pale. The smooth pale trunk goes up a long way; he can't guess how far it is up to the first branch. Maybe seventy feet, maybe eighty, maybe even a hundred. He had no idea that such trees existed.

Macpherson prompts.

'That's good. Now look around a little further. What else do you see? Or hear, or smell?'

Smell, yes. The smell of smoke. Not wood smoke, more like burning oil. And something else. A smell like burned meat. Charred black. Horrible. He pauses for a few moments, eyes still shut.

Of course. How can all of this have fallen out of his memory? He looks at the main section of the plane—or what is left of it. The wing on the near side has been ripped off completely, and most of the remnants of it are wrapped around one of the immense tree-trunks. Smoke is pouring out of jagged holes in the larger part of the fuselage, and a few flames, but nothing like the smoke and flames of half an hour earlier. The rear section is a short distance further away, clear of the fire. We were at the back and we escaped alive. The others—he can almost taste the harsh smell of the burning flesh now. And hear the roaring of the flames. And the screaming—the intolerable screaming. As if people are being torn apart into small pieces. It goes on and on. He doesn't know how long it is before the screaming finally dies away. He feels the horror of the pain, the terror of the others, trapped inside the mass of roaring flames and black smoke.

Macpherson interrupts the flow of memory. There is a more urgent tone in his voice than before.

'"We"'. You said "We have escaped alive". Who else is there?'

'There is a girl. A young woman.' Thomas stretches, finds a more comfortable angle for his legs.

'Does she have a name? Do you know her name?'

Thomas hesitates.

'Not at this moment. I only found out her name later.'

'Well, then. To be true to your memories we should for the moment just think of her as a young woman. But how do you come to be sitting against a tree?'

Thomas shuts out the immediate scene: the shelves packed with serious books, the big desk with the older man leaning forward over it. He has a vague memory of staggering away from the wreckage of the tail section, looking down and finding he is clutching his book, still open at the story of Saint Sabas. Of course. He was reading it in the plane when the engines abruptly cut out.

Cries for help come from the main section of the fuselage, but as he approaches it suddenly bursts into flames. For a few seconds he is unable to move, unable to decide what to do. The blaze flares up more fiercely. The calls for help change to agonised screams, but a blast of heat forces him to back well away.

As he circles around the wreck, frantically looking for an opening to make a rescue dash in, the fire swiftly engulfs the whole plane, dense black smoke churning skywards in an ominous column. He watches with horror as a face appears momentarily at one of the windows: a woman's face, surrounded by flames, hideously distorted by pain and terror, mouth open to let out an inhuman soundless shriek, silenced by the roar of the burning wreck. Then she disappears within the inferno. This is hell, he thinks, and she is trapped without any possible way out. His sense of helplessness becomes unbearable as does his certainty that he has to run for his life before he, too, is overwhelmed by the conflagration.

He reaches safety fifty or sixty metres from the disaster. With heaving chest and thumping heart, he drops to the ground behind a huge tree trunk, crouching, eyes tightly closed, hands over his ears, trying to shut out the dreadful reality. But there is no way of escaping the hideous mixture of smells from burning fuel, plane parts and human flesh. A long time later, he has no idea how long, he becomes aware that the noise has abated and the flames have subsided into a smoking tangle of wreckage.

Macpherson sits back in his chair, his eyes fixed on a point on the wall somewhere above Thomas's head.

'And the young woman. Where is she, and what is she doing?'

Thomas remembers finally opening his eyes, looking around and seeing her sitting on a log a few yards away. He can picture her quite distinctly, this first moment of focusing on her. She might be much the same age as himself. She is wearing a short-sleeved shirt, showing rather slight shoulders and arms. His attention is drawn to her legs. Weeping silently, she has pulled up her blue and white skirt a little way to rub her left leg, and winces as she rubs it.

An impulse comes over him to walk to her, to speak to her, to try to do something to console her. But what would be the right thing to do? Should he sit down close beside her? He should say something—but what? Should he put his hand on her hand, or on her shoulder, or an arm around both shoulders? He notices her hair—fair, and quite short. Should he touch her head? The situation is so far outside his experience. He can't make the first tentative move towards doing any of these things. He can't even imagine himself doing any of them. Someone else, yes, he can visualise that. But himself—he feels a paralysis of indecision.

Macpherson prompts. 'Please tell me about what happened next. Or what happens now: that is the way to think about it.'

Thomas sits back in his chair, closes his eyes, and takes himself back to the remembered scene. He is standing, feeling a tremor in his legs, taking shaky steps towards the rear section of the plane. There are two people—two bodies—among the twisted and torn debris on the ground between the sections of the fuselage. Are they complete bodies? He tries to turn away from them as he passes, but can't control the impulse to look. Confronting him are torn faces, heads caved in, half a leg, an arm missing, scorched, blackened. Blood. The horror is like nothing he has felt before. There is a churning nauseous feeling in his stomach. He looks away, trying to see no more, trying to control what he is feeling.

He clambers through the jagged opening into the tail section of the plane, looking for something. What is he looking for?

The rear seats, one on each side of the narrow aisle, are more or less intact. Behind the seats is a bulkhead with a narrow access door which has sprung open from the impact;

and behind the bulkhead is the baggage compartment. Cases, boxes and bags of various shapes and sizes, some intact, some split apart, spilling a jumble of clothing, shoes, belongings of all sorts, across the small space.

His own rigid black case has sprung open, disgorging grey and white striped pyjamas, spare collars, black socks, black trousers, white shirts, a black cardigan in case of cool south-coast weather, white underwear. They stand out against the jumble of brighter colours spilling out of other passengers' baggage: holiday clothes, mostly. He stuffs his own belongings back into the case and closes it, and continues rummaging through the confusion.

At the back of the small baggage compartment, under a scatter of clothing spilled from a split suitcase, something different appears: two rucksacks, well filled, with heavy walking boots tied to them. The preparations for a pre-Christmas hiking holiday that is not going to happen. He drags them out of the ruins of the plane and carries them back to the log on which the young woman is still sitting, moving them one at a time; they are heavy. He is anxious to sit on the log at an appropriate distance from her, but unsure what distance would be right. He picks a spot tentatively, a metre away, worrying that this might be too close. Putting the rucksacks on the ground, he sits on the log, and rubs his hands together between his knees.

She looks towards the smoking ruins of the plane and shudders. There are tears spilling down her cheeks.

'Those poor people.' She sobs, takes a deep breath, and steadies the tremor in her voice with an effort.

'What a terrible way to die. And us, being here, seeing, hearing everything—but no way to help.'

Thomas turns away from her, silent for a moment. 'I couldn't . . . I can't . . .'

He is unable to continue, unwilling to revive and confront in his mind the sights and sounds of horror, so turns his attention instead to the baggage he has retrieved.

The two begin sorting through the contents of the packs. The boots are too big to fit either of them. They pull out socks, men's underwear, shorts, shirts. Near the bottom of both packs some more basic essentials appear. Standard hiking rations: nuts, dried fruit, biscuits. And water bottles. Half a dozen small bottles in total, but only two of them are filled. He tries to estimate how long that much water will last. It will surely be finished tomorrow.

Thomas clambers back into the tail section of the plane to retrieve his own belongings as well as the young woman's travel bag. He returns to the log and they sit for a few minutes in silence.

She turns slowly to him, breaking the silence after a few moments of hesitation. Her voice is unsteady, almost inaudible. There is a sharp edge of fear in it.

'What can we do? Where are we? Do you have any idea? What direction could we go for help?'

Thomas shakes his head, looks around the small clearing where they are sitting. There are colossal trees in all directions; massive trunks in the foreground, and behind and between them more and more, receding into the background until any distant view is completely blocked out. The fear in her voice focuses his attention on their danger. Is it possible that he has survived the crash and the inferno to die slowly of thirst and exposure? The muscles across his shoulders are tense. The hairs on the back of his neck are standing up.

The crash site slopes up on one side towards the top of what must be a small hill. He stands abruptly, speaks abruptly. He'll walk up to the top of this hill. Possibly he'll see further afield from there. Maybe there are farms, or a house or at least something to give them an idea of where they are. He'll only be a few minutes.

He trudges up the slope, picking his way over long-fallen branches and around the buttressed bases of the enormous trees, aware of the awkwardness of his feet in their black, thick-soled shoes over the uneven terrain. However it's not a long climb, and the view from the top gives him at least a little of what he's been hoping for. One of the biggest of the trees has fallen, toppling down the other side of the hill, opening up a clear line of sight in that direction. Thomas looks out between the ranks of standing trunks on each side, and sees that the terrain changes suddenly and radically beyond the foot of the slope. The ground is flat, low-lying, covered with scrub rather than tall trees, stretching to a distant line of brilliant white marking the horizon. Coastal dunes. Here and there, where the line of the dunes dips lower, there are slivers of blue. The sea. He stands at the top of the hill scanning the scene fruitlessly for any sign of human presence. To left and right the low scrub is unbroken by cleared land or fences or buildings or roads as far as he can see. Wilderness. He shivers in spite of the warmth of the early summer afternoon.

Thomas picks his way back down the slope to where the young woman is still sitting on the log, rubbing her leg. She looks up at him, asks, with the same tense, sharp edge in her voice, what he found. Could he see any houses?

He shakes his head. No sign of people at all. But he could see through the trees to the sand dunes and the sea. At least they know they're near the coast.

He picks a slightly more distant place to sit on the log again, and stares for a few minutes into the cloud of smoke still escaping from the fuselage. Finally he turns towards her. Speaks hesitantly. He points out how little water they have. It will last them till, well, the next morning. No longer than midday. And they have to expect a warm day, maybe quite hot. There might be water on the low-lying land on the other side of the hill; there's certainly none here. If no help comes by the morning they'll have to move. Walk towards the sea. It's their best chance of finding more water. And finding other people too, if they follow the coast. At least it will give them a direction and save them from walking around in circles in this forest.

She looks away from him into the trees for a few moments, then turns back to face him. Thomas notices a couple of small wrinkles between her eyebrows. He wonders what they mean. She hesitates before responding. Walk to where? How far would they have to go?

He doesn't know how far. Has no idea. But they will have to try if help doesn't arrive soon. Either that or stay here and die of thirst.

She turns away, staring into the dimness between the trees. Speaks after a short silence. 'I suppose you're right. There's really nothing else to do. But I'm not sure how far I'll be able to walk.' She touches her leg cautiously, and winces. He glances at her leg and thinks he can see a bruise beginning to form, quickly looking away again, nervous in case she might think he was staring.

★

Thomas is sitting on the same log. The afternoon has dragged on towards evening. The sun, out of sight behind the treetops, must be low in the sky. The indistinct spaces between the trunks are fading gradually towards darkness, but there is still light in the clearing. The young woman is also there. They are both sorting through their belongings, deciding what to shift into the rucksacks. She has pointed out that they should be ready to move off early in the morning, before the heat of the day builds up.

The ground before each of them is strewn with clothing: his spare black trousers, white shirts and underwear, black shoes and socks, her skirts, blouses and dresses in clear, bright colours. He surreptitiously snatches an opportunity to glance across to where she has consolidated her underwear into a small heap, but it is hard to make out the forms of individual items. He looks quickly away as she begins to turn towards him to speak. There is not a great deal of room in her pack; she will have to leave a lot behind. And he will too, she supposes.

Thomas notices her eyes scanning the belongings spread out in front of him, focussing on a couple of spare clerical collars that he has put to one side, then moving up to the collar around his neck.

She pauses for a moment before speaking. 'I've been meaning to say—to ask. You're a clergyman of some sort.' Her rising inflection turns the statement into a question, calls for a response of some sort from him.

He stumbles over a reply. It's difficult to know how to explain. And embarrassing. A priest—a Catholic priest. No, that's not quite it, he's going to be ordained soon. He will be a priest in a month or two.

She nods. Yes, she thought something like that.

He looks away, thinking. Apparently she's a non-Catholic. A Catholic would understand that a Catholic priest could hardly be called a clergyman of some sort. To be a priest is to be unique, set apart.

She pushes the conversation in another direction, but one that prolongs his discomfort.

'This is silly,' she says, 'but we don't know each other's names. It looks as if we're stuck with each other for a while, so perhaps we should introduce ourselves. I'm Jane. Jane Peterson. And I'm a student teacher. I'm heading home to Albany for the Christmas holidays.' She attempts a shaky smile as she corrects herself. 'Perhaps I should say I *was* heading home. Heaven knows where we are heading now.'

He tries to match her half-smile about their predicament, and replies, 'I'm Thomas Riordan. And my family lives in Albany too. But it's years since I've spent much time there.'

The exchange feels uncomfortable for him. It's such an obvious and unchallenging thing to talk about, but his own contributions seem stilted, stiff. He can't remember a time when a young lady has spoken to him so freely and directly. In fact he can scarcely remember any conversation with a young lady at all. Even a trivial exchange like this feels like an excursion into unexplored country.

Thomas looks around the small clearing. The spaces between the enormous trunks, receding back into the depths of this remote forest, are getting darker. The light will be failing soon. They will need to be making whatever preparations they can for the night, and will need to get as much rest as they can. He worries about where the two of them might sleep. If sleep is possible after the horrors of the afternoon. Will she want him to be lying close, to let her feel just a little more secure in the lonely darkness? And if she does want him close, what will he do?

5

A Single Step

Macpherson holds up one hand. 'That is probably enough for today. We seem to be on the right track; the approach is working well so far. We'll continue next week with the following day's reading.'

He leans forward, focusing directly on Thomas' face.

'That—the plane crash and what happened to the victims—it must have been an overwhelming experience—a terrible thing for you to witness. To be there, almost in the middle of it all. It's not surprising that your mind shut the memories away. But now that we've managed to revive these sights and sounds they won't go away again. And there may well be more to come, possibly as confronting as these. You may need to develop ways of managing them so that you don't drown in them, so to speak. I'd like you to spend a few moments holding these memories in your mind, and then tell me what you are feeling about them.'

Thomas shuts his eyes, letting it all come up again: the half-dismembered bodies, the blood, the terrible, inhuman screams from within the inferno engulfing the fuselage, the inescapable, harsh smell of bodies burned black.

'It's all—it's nothing but horror.'

'Yes, it's to be expected that you would feel horrified by seeing and hearing other people suffering dreadful pain. It's part of what makes us human beings—at least normal, balanced human beings. I'd be rather disturbed if you *didn't* feel like this. But it's important not to be overwhelmed by the feeling.

'Notice that your whole body has stiffened, tensed, while these images flood in. Your muscles are all taut. Don't try to dismiss the sights and the sounds. Keep them in your mind, stay with them, but consciously relax all your muscles. Do it systematically, one part of your body at a time.'

Thomas has not noticed the tension building up in his body, or the fact that he has shifted forward to perch rigidly on the edge of his seat. He sinks back into the cavernous chair, closes his eyes, and consciously relaxes legs, arms, shoulders, neck, stomach muscles.

'That's fine, Mr Riordan. Now, do you find that makes it at least a little easier to bear confronting the memories?'

Thomas's reply comes after a pause of a few seconds.

'Yes. I can still picture the bodies and the flames and the rest. But I seem to be seeing it all from a bit further away, and I have a different feeling, if this makes sense. I've lost the feeling that it's all on the point of engulfing me.'

'Very good. Now I would suggest attempting a couple of extra strategies to manage the feelings. Try reminding yourself that these images and sounds are memories. You see and hear them as if they are happening now, but they are from the past. Focus on the thought that all that suffering is long over. Those people are beyond pain now. And there's one other way that's open to you, I imagine, though perhaps not to everyone. I take it that your religion involves believing in a loving God who is concerned for all his creatures—even a sparrow that falls, according to one text that I recall. Do you think that focusing on this belief might help you to control your response to these memories? It would suggest, I suppose, that whatever suffering people have undergone, God will arrange everything for the best in the end. Wipe all the tears from their eyes, as it's put somewhere.'

Thomas nods agreement, feeling some surprise to hear a self-confessed unbeliever referring to the scriptures, apparently familiar with them.

'Now are there any other feelings coming back as you recall that time after the plane crashed?'

The young man traces in memory the sequence of events that followed. 'Yes, there's something else. I'm not sure that I should go into it. The thing is it seems so trivial. I mean compared with what we've been talking about. It seems hardly worth mentioning.'

'Please tell me about it anyway.'

'When I think about being stranded down there, what I'm feeling, what I remember feeling . . . the memories are coming back to me now. You'd probably expect me to be afraid, not knowing where I was—terrified that I'd never find a way out. Maybe die there. There's some of that. But beyond that what I remember is the embarrassment, the sensation of awkwardness in my whole body, about the young woman being with me. About not knowing what to do—how to be so close to her.'

The young man looks up and sees a new level of intensity in Macpherson's attention. 'That is a very interesting reaction.

Not at all trivial, I suspect. Possibly quite important. We will probably come back to that in a later session.'

The older man sits back in his chair, hands behind the back of his head. 'In the meantime I want to move on to another issue. It might not seem relevant at first, but when I think about it there is a connection with what we've been discussing. I have to say that I found the story of Saint Sabas—intriguing. I take it that a saint is someone to be admired, perhaps taken as a model to be imitated.'

Thomas nods, looking away from the older man's face. Wondering what this is leading to.

'I didn't understand the story about the apple. Why would anyone admire him for stepping on the apple rather than eating it? If he'd thought of eating it but kept it for someone who needed it more, I see the point of admiring that. That is generosity, unselfishness. We all admire people like that. But crushing it under his foot, that's just negative, destructive, isn't it? He doesn't get the benefit of eating it, and neither will anyone else. It will be no good to anyone. As I see it, the world was a tiny bit worse off for what he did.' Macpherson shakes his head, looking puzzled. 'I'm not entirely sure why I'm talking about this. It's not really part of my brief, not my business, you might think. And you'd possibly be right. But I think it might turn out in the end to be relevant. Relevant, perhaps, to a rather different problem from the immediate one of your missing memories. But apart from that, this story is alien, I mean unfamiliar territory, to me. I'm intrigued. In a philosophical way, if you like. The thinking behind it puzzles me.

'And vowing never to eat another apple. Why would anyone admire that? What's the good of it? Who gets the benefit to set against his loss? If he'd vowed to grow apples to give to people who couldn't afford to buy them, then I see the point. The virtue, if you want to be formal about it. The goodness. The world would be better off for what he was doing. And all that self-inflicted starvation and thirst. What's the point there? Who benefits from it? He almost died of thirst. Is that supposed to be a good thing? Who was it good for?'

The doctor sits back in his chair looking up at the ceiling for a few moments. When his gaze swivels down again to Thomas his voice has a more decisive tone.

'While I'm speaking I'm beginning to get a clearer notion of what it was that disturbed me about your book. The author seemed to write about this man's suffering with an attitude of . . . I'm not sure how to describe his attitude. There's admiration there, certainly, which I don't understand at all, and something else. He seems to be fascinated by the man's pain. He celebrates it. There's none of the sympathetic human reaction that we were talking about earlier.'

He shakes his head again, but his expression and his tone lighten. He smiles his slight, controlled smile. 'Still, I think I worked out from the dates in the story that your saint lived well into his nineties. So it seems that all that self-inflicted torture didn't do him too much harm. Physically, at least.'

Thomas, still sitting back in the capacious leather chair, has been feeling the tension gradually building in the muscles of his shoulders and neck. Voices buzz in his head with words and phrases from a hundred sermons and homilies and readings. *Self-denial. Mortification of the flesh. I chastise my body and bring it into subjection.* He has never heard it questioned that this is saintly behaviour, pleasing to God.

This questioning, it's a voice from another world. There must be answers to all these questions. But among all the voices from his own world he can't find a response that he feels able to give to this man. He opens his mouth to reply but no words come.

Macpherson resumes, 'Let's spend the remaining few minutes trying a different approach. Dreams. I asked you last time to make a note of any dream that was vivid enough to make an impression on you. Have you had one over the week that you can describe to me?'

Thomas relaxes back into his chair a little. He can't see how this will help in the task of recovering his memories, but it doesn't seem so challenging.

'Yes. I had one a few nights ago that I can tell you about. It's a dream that I remember having before.'

'Very good. All the better probably, if it's a recurrent dream.' Macpherson sits back in his chair. 'Go ahead. I'm ready to listen.'

'In my dream I'm swimming. Or floating, really. I'm not actually moving through the water, though. I have the feeling that I'm out near the seminary, the first seminary I mean, when I was fourteen or fifteen. But nothing in my dream looks like the real place.

'The river is on one side of the seminary property; you may have driven past it. But the water I'm floating in is not like the river. Not at all. It's a long channel, fairly straight, as far as I can see. And narrow, I suppose only about . . . maybe twenty or twenty-five yards across. And the sides are nothing like the banks of the river: they're high and steep. Quite smooth too. As if they've been built. They're not natural.'

'I think I have a reasonably clear picture. That is the place. Now what is happening? Is anybody else there?'

'No, there's just me, the channel, and the water. I have no feeling of moving through the water. And there's no feeling that the water is flowing past me either. But then I notice something peculiar. I look at the high sides and I realise that I'm moving along the channel with the water—floating along without any sense of movement. It's completely silent too. But I've got a feeling that it's unstoppable.'

'Is there more? Do you have any sense of where the water is drifting you to?'

'I don't think there's anything ahead that's different from where I am now. There's just this slow flow. I'm just drifting along, wondering how I can get out, but the sides are high and steep, and I can't see a hand-hold or foothold anywhere.'

'And how do you feel about being in this situation? Are you afraid? Do you feel relaxed about it? What is your main sensation?'

Thomas considers the questions as he looks down at his hands, noticing faint scars, a reminder of his recent ordeal.

'I don't think I feel afraid. But I'm not really comfortable about it either. It's hard to explain—there's just this feeling that the water is in control, not me.' He looks up at Macpherson, sees that his eyes are closed, his head thrown back. And wonders what the doctor is making of this: what he can be thinking.

'Is it possible—are you able to explain what this dream means? Do you think that it might have some connection with the gap in my memories?'

The doctor's eyes open and he lowers his gaze to focus on Thomas. He pauses for a moment before answering.

'A connection with the gap in your memories—it is possible, not unlikely, I suppose. But I must spend a moment explaining something to you. I can't simply tell you what a dream means. Neither can anyone else. The meaning of a dream is the meaning it has for the dreamer—for you personally. I might be able to suggest ideas, but you must see the meaning yourself, perhaps with a few minor prompts from me. And it is likely to take a little time. I strongly suspect that this dream will turn out to have a meaning for you that's broader—more far-reaching than this problem of the missing memories.'

He looks at his watch. 'Ah, well. We will get back to the task next week. Another day, another saint, possibly another dream. In the meantime I would like you to spend a little time thinking about this dream. Ask yourself whether this image of yourself drifting along a channel with an imperceptible current is telling you something. You are being carried in a direction that you have no control over. Does this picture say something to you about your real life? Something important? Dreams are not usually about trivial things.'

Thomas, moving through the unkempt garden and out onto the street, turns Macpherson's last few words over in his mind. Drifting along with a current—how can this make sense in his waking life? The consultation has left him with a tight sensation in his belly, a feeling of uncertainty, insecurity, as if he has embarked on a long journey to an uncertain destination. The old proverb comes to his mind. *A journey of a thousand miles begins with a single step.* He has a sense that he has taken that single step. But where is the step taking him?

The question is abruptly swept aside. The images from the disaster, the shattered dismembered bodies, the surging flames, flood back into his mind, and with them the horror. He sits on the hard slatted bus stop seat and tries to relax his suddenly tense muscles, reaching for that sense of distance from the looming, threatening shapes and sounds.

6

The Word of God

Thomas slips into a pew near the confessionals. The congregation is beginning to trickle in for the second Sunday-morning Mass. He smiles, remembering Father Kevin's lengthy complaints last week.

'I don't know, m'boy. Why in God's name do they have to wait for the nine o'clock? If they all came to the seven o'clock it might be a bit of a squeeze, but we could get them out of the way in one hit. And I could get my breakfast at a reasonable time. I tell you, there's nothing much worse than waiting till half past ten to eat a couple of eggs that one of the nuns fried hard at half past eight and then left to go cold and greasy for a couple of hours. Like white and yellow rubber. You know, I reckon they do it on purpose. Pray God when you get a parish of your own it'll be one with a housekeeper, not nuns. Mind you, the average parish housekeeper is not a pleasant sight, in my experience. But the food is a hell of a lot better, even with the worst of them.'

Thomas pulls his thoughts back to the moment. These memories are too frivolous for this place. He looks up at the wall. One of the Stations of the Cross is above him: the image of Christ being stripped of his garments. The holy face has eyes turned up towards the heavens in deep shame at his body being exposed to the stares and taunts of the jeering bystanders. The holy head is crowned with thorns, and there are runnels of blood streaking the forehead and cheeks.

The image is instantly replaced by one from his memory: the area between the two sections of the wreckage of the plane. Runnels and splashes of blood on faces and bodies, torn-off limbs, blood pooling on the ground. The horror.

He tries to relax, to find again some separation from the threatening thoughts, to focus on the reality around him. Luckily, distractions arrive. An elderly man with grey thinning hair limps painfully down the side aisle and edges into the pew in front of Thomas, lifting his trailing leg in with both hands and arranging that foot beside the other on the kneeler. He has hardly managed to position his difficult limbs comfortably when Mrs Regan arrives down the same side aisle, leading a long procession of Regans of various sizes. She smiles deferentially at Thomas as she picks her way into the same pew, stumbling over her predecessor's feet. The man winces and tries to arrange his stiff legs more safely. The rest of the family follow, and he winces anew as each Regan squeezes and stumbles past him.

This must be the husband, with the bloated belly and the nose like a reddish potato. The girl with the glasses and the earnest expression must be Mary, destined for the convent, according to her mother. She looks the part already. More children straggle and stumble into the pew. Can these all be Regans? How many are there supposed to be? Father Kevin didn't seem entirely sure. A literary fragment pops up in Thomas's memory. *'What? Will the line stretch out to the crack of doom?'* Shakespeare, without a doubt. Which play, though? He should remember.

Mrs Regan eases herself down onto her knees, gropes in a bulky black handbag, and produces an unusually large set of rosary beads. She sets out on the familiar repetitive circuit of prayers in a loud, hoarse mutter: *'Our Father who art in heaven, hallowed be . . .'* Her beads generate a surprisingly loud rattle. How can rosary beads make so much noise? Thomas tries glaring at the back of her head. The mutter becomes even hoarser and louder. *'Holy Mary, mother of God, pray for us sinners now and at the hour . . .'* Then it fades back to its original level. Thomas sighs, resigns himself.

Father Kevin sweeps out into the sanctuary of the church, preceded by a small boy in red cassock and white surplice. The boy looks familiar. Of course; it's the Regan boy, Michael, the youngest altar boy in the parish, looking pinch-faced and worried. Behind him the small man is impressive, robed in splendid vestments embellished with gold. He seems to stand straighter in them. He even seems to have expanded his chest and shoulders to fill them. He is transformed.

Then, as the priest genuflects and mounts the two steps to the level of the altar, Thomas's attention is caught by the black bottoms of trouser legs and the thick-soled black shoes showing below the gorgeous robes. A pity, they take something away from the effect. What should priests wear on their legs and feet when they are robed for the altar? Certainly not black trousers and heavy black shoes. Bare ankles and sandals might look better. Though perhaps not in Father Kevin's case.

The priest stands, back to the congregation, facing the altar and behind it the grey back wall of the church, with its four narrow windows filled alternately with grubby plain glass and salvaged plywood. He intones the opening words: '*Introibo ad altare Dei.*' Thomas follows the familiar ritual, translating without effort: '*I will go in to the altar of God.*' And the ritual response comes, in the piping voice of the smallest altar boy: '*To God who gives joy to my youth.*' Michael is certainly youthful, but he doesn't look particularly joyful. Perhaps that anxious expression just runs in the family.

Mrs Regan's beads rattle, and her hoarse whisper rises for a moment above the liturgical Latin: '. . . *full of grace, the Lord is with thee, blessed art thou among* . . .' Then it fades down again to a background mutter.

Other sounds are competing for Thomas's attention. A series of low rumblings, snorts, wheezes. Somewhere close, ahead, off to the right a little. Mr Regan's head is wobbling, sagging sideways, jerking upright, starting again to wobble and sag.

Mrs Regan's hoarse muttering stops suddenly in mid-prayer. '*Holy Mary, mother of God, pray for*——' Her elbow darts out to dig sharply into her husband's ribs: 'Brendan! Wake up, Brendan. People will see you.' The voice is suddenly a sharp hiss, as sharp as the elbow. Mr Regan shakes his head and takes in a sudden, shuddering snorting breath. Then the muttering picks up precisely where it stopped: '. . . *us sinners now and at the hour of our death. Amen. Hail Mary full of grace, the Lord is* . . .'

Father Kevin descends the two steps from the level of the altar. He turns, embroidered robes swinging around the black-trousered legs, genuflects, and strides purposefully across to the pulpit, disappearing momentarily behind it. Among the congregation there is a collective relaxing and shuffling of feet and settling back on the hard seats of the pews. Mrs Regan stops her muttered prayers and turns to check on her husband. He is still apparently conscious, as far as can be seen from behind.

Father Kevin's head and upper body reappear as he mounts the pulpit steps and emerges above his flock. There is an outburst of deep, throaty coughing from the back of the church. He sets the priestly biretta level on his head, surveying the congregation, waiting for silence. The coughing, shuffling, muttering, all die down. It is odd how tall the short man seems to stand in the pulpit. Is it possible that he has something there to reinforce his authority: a small box perhaps, or a couple of telephone directories? Thomas imagines himself dressed in gorgeous robes, standing high above a congregation, waiting calmly for an attentive silence.

The priest begins: 'In the name of the Father, and of the Son, and of the Holy Ghost. Amen.' There is a faint mumble of response from the congregation. He taps the microphone standing on the pulpit rail. There seems to be no reaction, and he pushes the instrument aside. Not a bad thing, Thomas thinks. When it generates any sound at all it is mostly squeaks and squeals.

Father Kevin surveys the congregation again, glances down at his notes on the lectern, and declaims the text for his sermon:

'Go ye also into the vineyard, and I will give you what is just.' He pauses, sweeps his flock with his gaze, and repeats the text: 'Go ye also into the vineyard, and I will give you what is just. These words, my dear brethren, are taken from . . .' He hesitates, pauses, glances down at the lectern, peers, picks up the sheet of paper for a closer look. 'Taken from the Gospel of Saint Matthew, chapter twenty, verse four.

'My own words today are addressed first and foremost to the men among you: the workers, the husbands and fathers, the breadwinners, the householders. Yours is a noble calling. On your honest labour in the vineyard of life your families depend for food and clothing and shelter, and all the other necessities of life.'

He pauses, looking genially around at the men of the congregation. Thomas follows his gaze. The men are not very numerous, heavily outnumbered by the women. It always seems to be like that. Why would that be?

Father Kevin continues.

'You expect a fair day's pay for a fair day's work. And you are right to expect it. More than that, you are right to demand it. Otherwise how can your good wives and the little ones depend on you for a roof over their heads and clothes on their backs and food on the table?' He beams benevolently around at the good wives and their children.

From a couple of rows towards the back a piercing howl begins. Thomas takes a quick look around. A young, flustered mother is trying unconvincingly to pacify a small boy who has evidently reached the end of his tolerance for sermons, and is not only voicing his objections, but drumming his heels on the pew.

Father Kevin's genial beam disappears. The smooth rounded phrasing is replaced by sharp annoyance.

'Young woman, if you can't control that child I must ask you to remove him. The rest of the congregation came to hear the word of God.'

Thomas ponders. The word of God. He's not sure that the congregation has heard much of it up to this point. He looks around again. The mother is retreating towards the door, trying to make herself inconspicuous while dragging her little boy by one arm, still protesting and struggling.

As the disturbance recedes Father Kevin returns to the task. The benevolent glow lights up again on the narrow face under the priestly biretta.

'I was pointing out that you, the men of the parish, the breadwinners, are worthy of your hire. The late Holy Father of happy memory (his voice here takes on a reverential tone) made the Church's teaching on this aspect of social justice abundantly clear. That great Encyclical *Rerum Novarum* is a shining light for the whole world.'

He pauses, looks down at his notes again, and proceeds at a faster pace.

'A fair day's pay for a fair day's work. That fair day's pay my dear brethren, must do more than keep you alive, you and your families, in modest comfort. It must allow you, must it not, to maintain and even improve the tools of your trade. The carpenter must have the wherewithal,' he pauses, and repeats the splendid word with what sounds like justified satisfaction, 'the wherewithal to maintain a sharp saw and a serviceable hammer. The plumber needs his . . .' Father Kevin pauses, hesitates, his right hand reaching out and grasping at the air.

Thomas feels for him, scans his own memory for an image of a plumber at work with his tools of trade. What on earth do plumbers use? Nothing comes to mind, and nothing, apparently, to the small priest's mind either. He goes on rather lamely, 'the implements of his calling.'

Mrs Regan is rattling her rosary beads again. Her mouth moves steadily. The words are audible from time to time in her hoarse whisper. '. . . *us sinners now and at the hour of our death. Amen. Hail Mary full of grace the Lord is . . .*'

Her husband's head is drooping again. As far as can be seen from where Thomas sits his eyes are shut. His breathing is slow and steady, and emits a gentle rumble from time to time. Then for twelve or fifteen seconds it stops altogether, and restarts with a sudden loud snort. Mrs Regan's sharp elbow jabs hard into his ribs. He jerks suddenly upright with an even louder snort and looks around with a puzzled expression in his watery eyes. His wife's muttering continues uninterrupted. '. . . *art thou among women and blessed is the fruit . . .*'

Father Kevin pauses to glare at the snorter. The pause stretches out almost unendurably. The priest looks searchingly around the congregation with a sterner expression, appearing to be standing even taller above them.

'However,' he says. There is something arresting about his tone. Thomas sits up straighter on the hard pew. There is a sound of vague stirring among the parishioners, then silence. Mrs Regan's muttered prayers also fall silent. Mr Regan shakes his head vigorously.

'However, that is only one side of the issue. You have rights, but you also have duties. Grave duties. And the first and gravest of your duties is to God. To God and to the Church of God. Our holy mother, the Church, lays on you the obligation, as well as the privilege, to contribute to the support of your pastors and the dedicated nuns and brothers who devote their whole lives to God's work. And the Church speaks with the voice of God. I warn you my dear brethren, you are not hearing or heeding the voice of God.' Father Kevin glares challengingly around the congregation, eyes flashing, small chin thrust forward.

'And you ignore the voice of God at the peril of your immortal souls.' His voice reverberates off the walls and the ceiling.

Mr Regan is certainly awake now. He turns his head a little; there are very small beads of sweat on the side of his forehead. Mrs Regan's muttering begins again at a distinctly faster rate: '*for us sinners now and at the hour of . . .*'

The small priest moves on to more detailed material.

'The parish debt stands at seven thousand eight hundred and forty-six pounds five shillings and seven pence. As at last Friday morning. I must tell you that this is a little more than it was three months ago. And that figure was a little more than it had been six months ago. It is not merely that we are making no progress towards paying these buildings off. It is plain that the parish is sinking inexorably further into debt. Inexorably.' The word comes off his tongue impressively.

'And the reason for this is equally plain. The funds coming in to support the work of God from the Sunday morning Mass offerings are not growing as they should in a healthy parish. They are shrinking, slowly but surely. Is this what you owe to our Blessed Saviour, who gave every drop of his blood for your sake?'

For ten seconds or so he glowers at the congregation.

'No! You owe him a great deal more than this. And remember, the same Saviour is also the Judge who will return on the Last Day to call you to account. Think of that, my dear brethren, and think of being cast into the darkness outside where, as the Word of God tells us, there will be weeping and gnashing of teeth. And the fires of Hell.'

He pauses for a few moments. There is silence among the congregation apart from a momentary stifled cough from the rear of the church.

'I have not set out the full extent of our financial problems. The parish car is near the end of its long life. It is no longer reliable. We urgently need a replacement. I ask you, my dear brethren, to consider the heavy burden of guilt you would bear if a loved one of yours died without the last rites of our Holy Church because the old Austin failed to start in the middle of some winter night, and I was unable to answer the call. The difference between salvation and damnation for an immortal soul can rest on what happens in a situation of that sort.

'On another level, but no less important, the parish school needs equipment of all sorts. We should be in a position to spend money, not have to worry about repaying money we spent years ago. And there is the church window fund. As you know it was set up four years ago to raise money for proper church windows: stained glass, with angels and saints. I have imagined the raising of Lazarus for one. It would shame me and shame all of us if I explained how little progress that fund has made.

'The work of God is built on the work of men.' Father Kevin pauses, looks around the congregation, and repeats the sentence: 'The work of God is built on the work of men.' To Thomas's ear there's a note of satisfaction in the repetition. With some justification too; it is a nicely turned sentence. He must remember to jot it down for future use.

The priest resumes, 'All of this would be understandable if you were living in want. But this is far from the truth. Almost all of the breadwinners among you are in regular work.

You live in houses of your own, however modest. Many of you drive cars. You go to beaches and football matches. How many of you men would there be who never enjoy a glass of beer or a smoke, or put a few shillings on a horse, or buy a magazine? There is no sin in any of these necessarily, of course. Provided the magazine is a decent one, which I am obliged to point out some magazines are not, in these decadent times that we live in. But if you are spending money on your personal pleasures that you owe to the work of God and his holy Church, you are, my dear brethren, putting your immortal souls in mortal danger.' He pauses again, allowing time for that last phrase to have its proper impact, and repeats: 'immortal souls in mortal danger.'

He turns and disappears down the pulpit steps, to reappear striding towards the centre of the sanctuary, genuflecting, mounting the two steps to the level of the altar, resuming the familiar Latin ritual.

Thomas is impressed. A fine performance. A particularly striking conclusion. He must make a note of that last phrase: 'immortal souls in mortal danger'. He imagines himself making good use of it.

★

Thomas enters the presbytery dining-room, a cramped corner off the equally cramped kitchen, with a chrome-legged table topped with red Laminex. Father Kevin looks up from his late breakfast.

'Look at that, m'boy. Another pair of rubber eggs.' He holds one up impaled whole on his fork. 'As God is my witness, you could play tennis with this one. How do they do it? The cooks in hell must all be nuns, without a shadow of doubt. That shouldn't trouble you and me though. We're getting our eternal punishment here.' He bites off a large mouthful and returns the rest to his plate to paddle it in a pool of Worcestershire sauce.

With the mouthful of egg obstructing speech for the moment he looks up again at the younger man, his narrow head tilted to one side as he chews, swallows, and grins lopsidedly.

'And what did you think of the sermon? A devil of a lot of time and thought went into that, I don't mind telling you. Should put enough of the fear of God into them to top up the coffers a bit, don't you think? I wouldn't mind buying one of those Holdens, the new model. Supposed to have plenty of go in them. The old Austin's hardly got the power to pull a Christmas cracker.'

Thomas looks down at his feet for a moment. The new Holden. Yes, he's seen them.

Father Kevin nods, forks the rest of his first egg into his narrow mouth. One cheek bulges. The jaws move steadily.

Thomas watches, turns to go, hesitates, turns back and finally, speaks.

'I really came in to talk about something.'

The older man gulps down the large mouthful.

'Well then, sit down, m'boy. There's nothing so serious that you have to stand up to talk about it. What's on your mind?'

'At that nine o'clock Mass, I was behind the Regans.'

'Of course you were. I saw you. What about it?'

'I couldn't help seeing, you know, hearing. Mrs Regan, she was rattling through the rosary most of the time. Hardly stopped. She paid no attention at all to the Mass. And Mr Regan, he was asleep far longer than he was awake.'

'So what's the problem?' Father Kevin has some difficulty forcing the question through another mouthful of egg. He chews vigorously, then swallows.

'You've got something against people saying the rosary? I remember what it was like in Ireland in the old days, thirty years ago or so. Especially out in the countryside. Most of the women used to say the rosary right through the Mass. Never faltered. Fast as they could go. Sometimes you couldn't hear yourself think for women muttering the Hail Marys. Wonderful piety in the old country. Did them a power of good, I'm sure.

'What else was worrying you? That's right. Brendan Regan dropping off all the time. You mustn't blame Brendan. I think I told you he's a barman down at the Shamrock. Finishes up late every night except Sundays. But he's up at five most mornings helping Brian O'Halloran with the training. Brian's got three or four horses running. Brendan works like a dog to feed that tribe of kids. No wonder he needs his sleep. He's a good man for a tip on the gallopers by the way, if you're interested. I should have mentioned it. Falling down on my responsibilities.'

Thomas hesitates. 'Yes, but . . . people like that. Most of them I suppose. They can't follow the Latin. There's nothing for them to do. You see, I suppose I'm starting to wonder why we stick with it, the Latin I mean. Maybe it would make sense to do it all in English. Then everyone could—what's the word—participate.'

Father Kevin looks hard at him, fork poised in front of his mouth with the last chunk of generously sauced egg lodged precariously on it.

'Participate!' He lowers the fork to the plate and sits back. Thomas feels uncomfortable under his gaze, and looks down at the floor, rubbing his hands together between his knees.

'Where are you getting these ideas from, m'boy? You should know better than I do what the Church teaches about this. The Mass isn't a social occasion, it's a sacrament. The priest celebrates it, the laity attend. You don't need me to tell you all this. And the Latin keeps up the tradition, holds everything steady, the way it's always been. People like the Regans, they don't have to understand it all. Better in a way if they don't. It keeps them in mind of the mystery and magic.' He looks obliquely at Thomas and grins slyly. 'And the fact that they need the priest to work the magic for them.

'So you noticed that Brendan Regan slept most of the time. He does it every Sunday. It doesn't really matter, or it wouldn't if he stopped letting out those terrible loud snorts. He's there, that's all that's needed from him. If he was awake there wouldn't be anything much for him to do. We do it for him. Or I do, and you will when you're given the powers.

'You worry me, boy. These are Protestant ideas you're playing with. Those Protestant pastors, I'm told you can see them after their services socialising with people, shaking hands and asking after the health of everyone's aunties and grandmas. Handing cups of tea around. Ridiculous. They wouldn't know what a sacrament was if one came up and bit them on the backside. But you—you should know better. What do they teach you young fellows in the seminary these days?'

Thomas looks down at his feet again, feeling awkward. 'It's not the seminary. It's just that . . .' He pauses, unsure how to go on.

Father Kevin doesn't wait.

'We'll say no more about it then. And I won't mention it to the archbishop. Anyway this stuff is too serious to talk about after Mass on a Sunday morning. What do you reckon on doing between now and Benediction? A young fellow like you should be looking for a bit of healthy exercise, not tormenting himself and his elders with questions that better men than either of us settled centuries ago. They have those tennis courts over at the Brothers' school. You play, I suppose? So do some of them. It'll do you a power of good. Blow away the cobwebs. Take the Austin after lunch. It should make the distance. You'll never get a bus on a Sunday afternoon.'

7

The Feast of Saint Bibiana

Thomas sits back in the deep leather chair. He closes his eyes and focuses on relaxing his muscles, one body part at a time, consciously attending to the sensations in his toes, ankles, calves, stomach, shoulders, neck. Like everything, he is finding, it gets easier with a little practice.

Macpherson watches approvingly.

'I see that you've been working on the skill of relaxation. I imagine that the sights and sounds of the plane crash have been coming back to you at times over the week. It must be disturbing when they do. Inevitably. Have you found the relaxation exercise useful to keep your reactions under control?'

Thomas opens his eyes to respond.

'Yes, but there's something else. I'm not sure how this might sound, to you I mean.' He feels the muscles of his neck and shoulders begin to tighten.

'We won't worry about how it might sound to me. Try to relax again and tell me about it.'

'It was at the cemetery last Wednesday. A funeral. I went with the parish priest. Beside the new grave, suddenly it all came back. You know, the horror, the torn pieces of body and the smashed heads. The roaring flames, and the screaming. The hideous screaming was worst of all. I felt as if it was tearing something apart inside my head.'

He pauses, shakes his head as if to shake some of the horror loose.

'And I looked around to focus on something else—you know, anything different from what I was seeing and hearing in my head. There was a tombstone there. And written on it were the words, *Sleeping Peacefully*. It seemed to help. Just looking at the words, and imagining those people sleeping peacefully. I felt more peaceful myself.'

'That's interesting. As far as I can see you are managing those traumatic memories well. Perhaps we could go on with our strategy. I see that you've brought the book. Who is our saint for the day? The second of December, if I can trust my notes from last week.'

Thomas leafs through the pages. 'December the Second. The Feast of Saint Bibiana, virgin and martyr. 363A. D.'

'Well, now. Saint Bibiana. Another stranger to me. And an ancient one. Let's hear about her. Remember to be alert for any memory that comes to mind from the last time you read her story.'

Thomas sits back with his book and begins.

We are informed by Ammianus Marcellinus, a pagan historian of that age, and an officer in the court of Julian the Apostate, that this emperor made Apronianus governor of Rome in the year 363, who, while on his way to that city, had the misfortune to lose an eye. This accident he superstitiously imputed to the power of magic, through the malice of some who excelled in that art; and, in this foolish persuasion, to gratify his spleen and superstition, he resolved to punish and exterminate the magicians; in which accusation Christians were involved above all others, on account of many wonderful miracles which were wrought in the primitive ages. Under this magistrate, Saint Bibiana received the crown of martyrdom.

This holy virgin was a native of Rome, and daughter to Flavian, a Roman knight, and his wife Dafrosa, who were both zealous Christians. Flavian was apprehended, deprived of a considerable post which he held in the city, burned in the face with a hot iron, and banished to Acquapendente, then called Aquae Taurinae, where he died of his wounds, a few days after. Dafrosa, by order of Apronianus, who had thus treated her husband for his constancy in his faith, was, on the same account, confined to her house for some time; and, at length, carried out of the gates of the city, and beheaded.

Bibiana and her sister Demetria, after the death of their holy parents, were stripped of all they had in the world, and suffered much from poverty for five months, but spent that time in their own house in fasting and prayer. Apronianus had flattered himself that hunger and want would bring them to a compliance; but, seeing himself mistaken, summoned them to appear before him.

Demetria, having made a generous confession of her faith, fell down and expired at the foot of the tribunal, in the presence of the judge. Apronianus gave orders that Bibiana should be put into the hands of a wicked woman named Rufina, who was extremely artful, and undertook to bring her to another way of thinking. That agent of hell, employed all the allurements she could

invent; which were afterwards succeeded by blows: but Bibiana,
making prayer her shield, was invincible.

Apronianus, enraged at the courage and perseverance of a
tender virgin, at length passed sentence upon her, and ordered her
to be tied to a pillar, and whipped with scourges loaded with leaden
plummets till she expired. The saint underwent this punishment
cheerfully, and died in the hands of the executioners. Her body was
left in the open air, that it might be a prey to beasts; but, having
lain exposed for two days, was buried in the night, near the place of
Licinius, by a holy priest called John.

Thomas shuts the book, puts it aside and looks up to find Macpherson's eyes on him.

'That's not a long story, but it's certainly a remarkable one in some ways. We'll return to that later. For the moment there are more pressing matters. When you last closed the book on that story, where were you? Or rather, where are you? What is happening around you?'

Thomas closes his eyes. Images and sensations start to float into his consciousness. He is putting the book down on fine white sand. Looking over his shoulder he finds that he is sitting at the foot of a high dune, with his back against the steep slope. The surface of the sand has been warmed by the increasing heat of the morning, but when he pushes that layer aside there is a pleasant coolness against his back. With any slight movement, small runnels of sand slide down the slope. He picks up the book again to return it to the rucksack that is resting beside him, and takes out a water bottle for a drink. It has an unpleasant, muddy taste. The bottles had been filled from a small creek running through a low-lying area.

The water was brownish, like weak tea, and smelled of mud and decaying leaves. Tiny fish darted away for shelter in tangles of fallen leaves and branches as he dipped the bottles into one of the deeper pools.

From the other side of the dunes, Thomas can hear the soft thunder of waves breaking on a beach. The sound has been creeping gradually nearer through the morning's trek towards the coast. Before him is the stretch of country across which they have struggled to find a way: an expanse of fairly flat land densely covered with scrub, mostly about eight or ten feet high. At this distance the scrub is a uniform dull grey-green. Seen close up most of the shrubs have small leaves and tiny white flowers. When a branch was shaken as he passed, a shower of delicate petals drifted down and settled on his shoulders. Here and there are bushes with bigger leaves and bright red bottle-brush flowers that stand stiffly upright. Away in the background is the higher ground from which they have come: a line of hills that stand up steeply out of the low flat land between. The hills are crowded with towering trees: massive, smooth trunks with high branches that he sees, from this distance, as arms reaching up, dividing into clumps of leaves like thickened fingers. And, somewhere among those hills and trees, the shattered remains of a plane, and the scattered burnt remains of its occupants. A small smudge of what looks like smoke among the deeper green tree tops suggests the location.

Macpherson intervenes: 'And the young woman? Where is she? You have a name for her now I think, according to my notes. Should she be Jane, or Miss Peterson?'

Thomas scans the scene. She is there sitting beside her rucksack, a few yards away along the foot of the dune, leaning back against the steep sand incline. Her eyes are closed. She looks exhausted. Seeing her resting, vulnerable, he thinks of her as Jane.

She has struggled with the walk from the crash site, limping from the pain of her deeply bruised leg, pushing through the scrub. Once a branch had whipped back after Thomas had passed ahead of her, and caught her in the face. He heard her cry out and turning back, realised his carelessness. At the time he said nothing. Perhaps he should have said something, but what?

They have had to detour around patches of swamp, tripping on roots and stumps. She has sometimes fallen too far behind and had to call to him, ask him to wait.

'Please. I can't walk so fast.' Her pack, with food and water bottles and spare clothes and shoes is too heavy for her. He has had to wait for her to catch up. Several times. When they stopped beside the creek to refill the water bottles he had been anxious to press on promptly, but she wanted to sit with her back against the stem of one of the bigger shrubs and have what she called a proper rest. He had to sit down too, chafing about the loss of time.

It was during that rest stop that she turned to him with a series of questions. They followed each other as if she had been turning them over in her mind for some time. A priest, she said, a Roman Catholic priest would have to stay single, celibate, is that right? He agreed, wondering at the same time why she would want to press him about this. She turned the questions in a much more personal direction. Why would anyone, she began, why would he want to do that? Wouldn't he want to marry, have a wife and a home of his own? A family? In time, of course. It's what most people imagine themselves doing.

He found her questions confronting. A kind of invasion. Another Catholic wouldn't have asked him these questions, would have understood that a priest commits himself not to do what most other people do. What reason would she have for interrogating him like this? He noticed her puzzled expression while she listened to his hesitant attempt at an explanation.

Finally, after that rest by the watercourse, she was ready to move on. But it must have been only half an hour later that she stopped to look at a flower, calling to him to come back to see it. An orchid, she exclaimed. It was nothing special: a spidery thing close to the ground, hardly noticeable. It took much longer than it should have done to get this far, to the beginning of the dunes.

Now he stands, swinging his own pack up onto his shoulders. They must move on. Over the sand-hills to the coast. It's the only way to find an escape from this wilderness.

She crouches, twists her body to get the straps of the pack over her shoulders, lurches forward onto hands and knees and struggles to stand. He waits until she is upright, then turns and tackles the steep face of the dune. The sand is soft and loose. His feet sink deep into it as he slogs laboriously up the slope.

Half-way up he hears her call from behind and below.

'Wait. Please, Thomas. For me.' He turns, plods down the slope again, feet sinking and sliding, and stops a couple of yards short of the bottom.

She is looking up at him. Tears are running down her cheeks. She can't do it. The pack is too heavy. Her leg is really painful after they have walked so far. Her feet are sinking into the sand. She will never get to the top.

Thomas looks down at her. When did a young woman last address him by name? When did one speak to him at all? He notices again how slender she seems. How slight her shoulders and arms. How strange, that these made no lasting impression on him until now. And the bruise down the side of her leg, or as much as he can see of it below her skirt—he hasn't really noticed before how big and dark it is.

Sliding down the last of the slope, Thomas hoists the pack off his shoulders. She sits and shrugs hers off with an effort. He sits too, confused, undecided. What is to be done? What can they do? Eventually, he has a suggestion. Perhaps she can stay here. He can go on alone and try to get help back to her when it is possible.

She looks around.

'Stay here? In this place? By myself? For how long?' She is silent for a long while. The surf booms from the other side of the dunes. She shivers.

Finally she turns towards him with another suggestion, sounding tentative, apologetic. Perhaps her rucksack could be left behind. If they left behind everything but the absolute essentials. Food and water bottles. If they shifted those into his pack. Perhaps he might be able to carry the load for both of them. She is sorry, but she doesn't think she can go any further with weight on her back. But she can probably climb this hill and go on without this burden.

Thomas feels a moment of resistance. Then he considers. Perhaps it's possible. They begin to discard spare clothes, shoes. He looks at the clerical collars that have come from the bottom of his pack. Glances across at her, remembering her eyes focusing on them the previous afternoon. He pushes them aside. After a moment's thought he unfastens the collar from round his neck and drops it with the others. They shift food and water into his rucksack. He tries the weight. It is heavier, but not impossible. He looks at *Lives of the Saints*, considering, deciding that for him this is one of the real essentials. He stuffs the book back in, between sultanas and peanuts, hoists the pack onto his shoulders, and takes two or three short steps up the face, his feet sinking deep in the loose sand. Jane calls from behind. He turns back, sees her outstretched hand. Can he help her?

'Please, Thomas, just a little.' She's sorry. Her leg. This hill is very hard for her, even without the extra weight.

He reaches out with his right hand, takes her left hand in it, feeling a tense, prickly feeling across his neck and shoulders as their hands touch. There is an urge to withdraw, to pull back into himself. Her hand grips his more firmly. With the pressure of her grip his whole body is taken over by a surge of arousal that he can do nothing to control or conceal. He prays that she will not notice, trying to stay a little ahead of her as they trudge laboriously, hand in hand, up the steep face of the sand-hill under the heat of the mid-day sun.

At the top a revelation is waiting: a vast expanse of ocean stretching out to the horizon, transparent turquoise close to the shore, shading to deep opaque blue in the distance. Streaks and flecks of white foam chase each other across the surface. Long swells are peaking and curling over slowly and breaking white on a long beach. Away in the distance in both directions the sand ends in rocky headlands. Between where they stand and the shore there is a series of lower dunes: brilliantly white sand, unmarked except for small wind-formed ripples. A few patches of coarse pale-grey grass are growing through the sand. A light breeze from the sea makes the grass clumps ripple and sway.

Thomas remembers feeling more sharply at the top of that high dune, the prickly discomfort of holding her hand, standing so close. The embarrassing physical excitement. He withdraws his hand and takes a short step to face away, applying his attention to scanning the beach and the sea for any signs of other people. But there are none.

The two, walking further apart, head down the more gradual seaward slopes towards the shore, in the coolness of the sea breeze drifting inland. The beach drops quite steeply down into the surf. Successive rollers rear up, peak, and curl over to crash down onto the sand, sweeping white foam up the slope, throwing up clouds of fine spray that drift towards them as they walk down the seaward face of the last dune.

Thomas stares along the shore as far as the next headland in both directions. There is no sign of human presence. He feels a sudden sense of helplessness—of falling into an infinite, featureless space from which there is no possible escape. His head seems to be spinning.

Jane too has been scanning the beach in both directions. She turns towards him.

'This place. This piece of the coast. I know the coastline east and west of Albany for quite a long way; my family has had dozens of picnics and camping weekends at different spots. This is nowhere near Albany. I've no idea where we are. Can you recognise anything we've seen?' The sharp edge of fear is in her voice.

Thomas shakes his head, spreading his empty hands out.

'There's nothing here I recognise, no way of working out where we are. I don't know what we can do.'

Recalling Saint Euthymius and Saint Sabas in the desert, he makes a silent plea for divine guidance, but none comes. Thomas sits on the sand, trying to control the dizzy sensation of falling into empty space.

His mind is suddenly invaded by memories of the wrecked plane: the flames and black smoke, the roar of the inferno, the frightful screams of the victims trapped within it and that terrified face at the window. He tries to turn his attention elsewhere, to shut the memories away, to focus on the realities around him: the beach, the sea, the distant headlands, Jane.

She sits beside him, a little too close for him to feel comfortable. Her skirt slips up above her knees for a moment before she smooths it down again. He notices before he turns his eyes away that her thighs seem more substantial than he would have expected from the lightness of her arms and shoulders. Is this usual for women? They both stare out across the breakers to the horizon.

She speaks again, after several minutes. Her voice sounds firmer, more purposeful.

'I've been thinking, trying to work out where we are. I've made this flight once before. The road trip, too, a few times. The plane follows much the same line as the road. It should do anyway, but in our case it didn't. I was waiting to see the Stirlings, you know, the mountains. We should have passed quite close, and I always look for them as a sign that I'm nearly home. I caught a glimpse of the peaks not long before the plane crashed. But it was just a glimpse; they were tiny spots far away on the horizon. They should have been almost beside us.

We were a huge distance off course, heaven knows how far. This place here, it must be miles and miles beyond Walpole.'

She is silent for a few moments. When she speaks again her voice is subdued, less confident. The edge of fear has crept back into it.

'This is not a good place. To be stranded, I mean. A big stretch of empty land. No farms, no roads, nothing. Nothing that we need, anyway. I don't know what we can do. What do you think?'

Thomas, listening, has been taken over by a sense of inadequacy. Isn't it a man's role to be knowledgeable, authoritative, in control? What has he to contribute? Nothing except his first thought of the previous afternoon.

'We don't have many options. There's no point in going back into the forest. We'll just have to go along the coast and hope to find . . . something. Somebody. The only question is which way: left or right. Which makes better sense?'

She sits silent for some time, staring one way and the other along the shore. Thomas glances at her momentarily, and notices the beginning of sunburn on her nose and cheeks. The pink areas stand out against her fair skin. Eventually she speaks, her voice a little unsteady.

'I don't know, I'd be guessing. If we go left the first place we get to is Walpole. But I don't know how far it is. A long way, definitely. And if we're following the shore, we might even miss it. There's nothing right on the coast there. The town is some distance in from the coast. Going the other way, I'm not sure. There's nothing like a town for miles. Much further than Walpole. But I've heard about a little collection of fishing huts somewhere on the coast in that direction. Which one is closer—I've no idea. They could both be a few days away if we're walking.' She tries to force a half-smile. 'And I can't see any other way of getting there. Left or right—it's a toss-up as far as I can see. So there's an idea. It's the only one I have. We have no way to decide which way to go. What about flipping a coin?'

Thomas looks away from her for a moment, feeling uncertain. Could this be seen as having a taint of superstition about it? A suggestion of consulting an oracle? Probably not. He feels relieved that the responsibility for the decision is not his.

He reaches into his pocket and brings out a two-shilling coin. Heads, we go right; tails, we go left. He tosses it in the air, watching it spinning, anxiously aware that their fate, either safety or disaster, might be resting on the chance outcome of the spin.

Jane drops to her knees over the coin where it lands on the strip of beach washed smooth by the waves. She looks up at him.

'Heads. We go right.'

They both turn, looking along the beach towards the next headland. Through the faint mist drifting in from the breakers it looks a huge distance away: a vague darker shape looming above the end of the beach. They both stand silent.

★

Thomas opens his eyes to see Macpherson closing his notebook and leaning forward across his desk.

'That's fine. Excellent, in fact. I think we should leave the story for today. But perhaps we might explore one or two details that have come to light. I was interested in what you said about your reaction to touching the young lady's hand. An awkward, prickly feeling, I think you said. An urge to withdraw, to pull away.'

Thomas nods, looking down.

Macpherson puts his notebook aside and continues, 'It's a—what should I say—an unusual response in a young man. Most of us, at your age, would probably have found it rather a pleasant experience. The physical response too, though I understand that you might not have wanted it to be obvious.'

Thomas shifts forward to the edge of his chair. He clasps his hands together between his knees. Some of that same sensation is coming back: the prickly feeling in his head and neck and shoulders, the urge to withdraw. He can't meet the older man's eyes. What does this have to do with the recovery of his memories?

Macpherson waits, rubbing his cheek with his hand, but no response comes. When he speaks he sounds tentative.

'This is perhaps a side issue. But I would like to pursue it a little further, if you have no objection. Your plan to become a Roman Catholic priest—that would call for celibacy of course.'

Thomas nods.

'Yes.'

'And I believe you explained to me earlier that the training institutions occupied most of your time. I think you said that apart from the usual holidays you hardly left them at all.'

Thomas nods again. His mind flicks back to a memory from his first year at the seminary, and the first time he was permitted to leave as an individual for a day. It was for his grandfather's funeral, which had followed several years of increasing dementia in a Perth nursing home. The rector often advised his students to think about death, about their own deaths. A wedding in the family was of no great importance, but a funeral was an occasion not to be missed: a salutary reminder of mortality. He suggested never passing the local undertaker's establishment without looking into the corner window where a sample coffin was on display, and imagining themselves inside it.

Thomas remembers feeling detached from the funeral's ritual and the family's sorrow. The old man of his memories, in the old country town, with his garden, his summerhouse, his monkey-puzzle tree and his snapdragons, had gradually slipped away into a fog.

Macpherson calls him back to the task in hand.

'I see. A semi-enclosed establishment. And this would be an all-male institution.'

'Of course. All the students, and the teachers, lecturers. All men. Or boys, among the students. There are some nuns who do the cooking and cleaning, and so on. But we hardly have any contact with them. None, really.'

Macpherson leans forward, looking more intently at Thomas.

'Boys. Together with men. That is interesting'. He sits back in his chair and breathes out. 'So you have spent nine years from the age of fourteen in an all-male institution, with a view to being a celibate. And that was after years spent in another all-male institution, during school hours at least. Obviously holding a young woman's hand was going to be a very unfamiliar experience for you. But why would it be an uncomfortable experience? Why the urge to pull away? Why would it not have been an unfamiliar pleasure? Can you shed any light on this for me?'

Thomas looks down at the floor, searching in his mind for a response that he might be able to offer. A pleasure attached to close contact with a young woman—surely any such pleasure would fall within a vaguely understood but extensive range of pleasures that are sinful. Except, of course, in marriage, and then only within stringent limits. How can he explain all of this to a man who apparently doesn't deal with the idea of sin?

The older man pursues the issue.

'I would like you to consider this thought. Is it possible that your discomfort arose from a deep-seated sense of guilt that you feel about anything of a sexual nature? This is not a question to answer now. It's one to take away and think about. To think about in relation to what you have been taught over all those years.' He looks up at the ceiling for a few moments, and sighs. 'Perhaps this is not altogether my business, but on a slightly more practical level, do you think that spending nine years of adolescence and early adult life out of touch with people of the opposite sex would put anyone in a good position to decide whether he wanted to be a celibate for the rest of his life?'

Thomas considers, wonders whether this question really calls for an answer, and if so, what answer can he give? He can think of nothing to say.

Macpherson sits back, taking another line.

'Your saint for the day, who was she?' He glances down at his notes. 'Saint Bibiana. That was a—what can I say—an intriguing story. To me, I mean. Intriguing from a professional point of view. I was struck by the emphasis on pain. Suffering. There seemed to be some sort of fascination with it. People dying in quite horrible ways. Is that why this young lady was a saint: because she died in a horrible way? Flogged to death with whips loaded with lead weights. It's a hideous image. But any number of people have horrible deaths, one way and another, poor souls. Every week. Every day. Are they all saints?'

Thomas is still perching awkwardly on the edge of his chair. His neck and shoulders still feel locked tightly in position, hands stiffly curled on his thighs. How can he explain so that this man can understand?

'It's not just the pain. She was a martyr. She died for her faith. She refused to renounce Christianity. That's the reason.'

Macpherson rubs the side of his face with a finger. He still looks dubious.

'I see, perhaps. Perhaps I can follow that, up to a point. So people who die because of accident, or carelessness, or stupidity, or something like that—they're not saints, no matter how unpleasant their ends might be.'

He pauses.

'But I'm still a little puzzled. This young lady who died for her faith, apparently she is to be admired. I still don't grasp why. What good did her dying do for anyone? If she had told a few lies to the governor to get out of that awkward situation so that she could stay alive and carry on running her soup kitchen for the destitute behind the Colosseum, I would admire that. And if I thought that a God existed I might imagine that God would admire it too. Depending on what sort of God I had in mind. Because she would have been relieving some of the suffering in the world. As it was she just added her own suffering to what was there already. Why would anyone admire that? Even if it were for the faith.'

Thomas feels all his joints locked tight. His mind also. There are answers to these questions. There must be answers.

But he scans his memory and finds none. And he has fallen, somehow, into a situation where there is no authority to refer to. He must find his own answers, but he can't see where answers might be found. He is relieved when the doctor moves to another approach.

'Perhaps we should put those issues aside for the time being and think for a while about your dreams. The dream you described to me at our last meeting about floating down a channel between two high banks—I take it that you have been thinking about it from time to time. I don't want to discuss that just now, or what you have made of it. I want you to hold it in mind, and, keep considering what it might mean. But what about this last week? Have you had any memorable dreams over these few days?'

Thomas relaxes back into his chair.

'Yes, there is one. I dreamt that I was out at the seminary—the first one I went to. Though what I saw there was rather different from the reality——'

The older man intervenes.

'That's interesting. Your previous dream was set there, too. That's something for you to think about. But go on, please. Tell me what is happening there.'

'In my dream there's a very thick high row of shrubs along the front boundary of the property. Like a hedge. But it's uneven and tangled, not trimmed and neat. I'm walking along beside this line of unkempt bushes. At Saint Aloysius there really is a line of shrubs grown together along the front of the property. I remember when I was there noticing one day the scent of the flowers on some very old rose bushes that were tangled up in it. But the shrubs in my dream are higher and thicker. I'm wandering along beside this hedge. And I know in my dream that I've often wandered along beside it in my waking life. But I see something that I've never noticed before. There's an old gateway in the middle of it. There're no gates, but the gate posts are connected by a sort of arch. It's overgrown with branches and creepers—can't have been used for many years—but it's still obvious enough. I'm puzzled about why I've never noticed it before.'

Macpherson waits for a moment before replying.

'An interesting dream. You might want to think about what gateways are for: we go in through them, and we go out through them. Is it likely that this dream is an expression of thoughts and feelings that are brewing, so to speak, in your mind, but well below the level of consciousness? Ideas and feelings about going in somewhere, or going out from somewhere. Possibly even both. And in your dream the way through is blocked by thick shrubbery; that must mean something. But don't be too literal in your thinking; remember that dreams are usually symbolic. Like the first, this one may well have something to tell you.'

He glances at his watch, pushes his chair back from the desk.

'We'll leave it until next week and maybe I'll hear about a different type of saint. Possibly a different type of dream.'

8

An Ecumenical Encounter

Thomas steps off the bus. Moving out from its shadow he feels the weight of the afternoon sun pressing down on him. The sea breeze has not arrived, the heat has built up through the day, and the north-easterly is still blowing, picking up flurries of dust and scraps of paper. The few juvenile trees throw no shade on the concrete slabs of the footpath. Sweat is trickling down his neck inside the stiff clerical collar, and the dead-black jacket is stifling. There is a twenty-minute walk to the presbytery ahead of him.

He sets off along the first block, trying to manage his thoughts. There are worse crosses to bear than a twenty-minute walk on a hot afternoon. He thinks of Saint Bibiana being flogged to death but refusing to renounce her faith. Would he have the courage and dedication to follow the saint's example of steadfastness? Probably not. But at least he can endure the discomfort of the stifling collar and jacket with a good grace, offering it as a small sacrifice to atone in some slight way for the sins of the world, his own included. Still, the sweat trickling down his body and soaking his shirt keeps intruding on these pious thoughts.

Two young men about his own age, wearing nothing but shorts and singlets, hurry past him in the opposite direction, switching between a fast walk and a jog while chatting about a cricket match. They seem to be so much at ease in themselves and the day that Thomas feels a stab of envy.

He remembers Macpherson's questioning. Why would anyone imagine a God who wants people to suffer? Why would a creator be better pleased with him, sweltering and sweating inside his clerical garb than with those two jogging freely and comfortably through the heat of the afternoon?

In the next block he looks for the house where the young mother was playing with her little boy a couple of weeks earlier. It's like a dozen other houses in the same street, except for its distinctive front door. His memory holds a sharply etched image of it closing, shutting her off from his view.

There it is, the drab little house with the bright red door and the small square of garden at the front. And there is the woman, further back from the street this time, in the narrow space between the house and the side fence. She is holding a hose again, watering some shrubs against the wall of the house. Hydrangeas. Thomas remembers them from his grandfather's garden, and some talk at a long-ago family Christmas celebration about how they need the water 'kept up to them' in summer. The mother is playing the same game with her little boy, who is getting nearly as much water sprayed on him as the plants. But this time he is stark naked. Is that decent? Perhaps it is innocent, in the case of such a young child. But where did that initial moment of shock come from, that Thomas felt on seeing him? Of course the toddler's nakedness is innocent. How could anyone think otherwise?

But the woman is not far short of naked herself. Her back is turned to the street and Thomas can't prevent himself from slowing his walk, stopping, staring at the female body in the sketchy two-piece bathers. A bikini. He remembers the archbishop's article in *The Catholic View* a few weeks earlier about bikinis, the threat such immodest garments posed to the purity of family life. His eyes follow the curves of her form: in at the waist, out at the hips, the rounded buttocks, the smooth thighs. Presumably she is a wife—a married woman—and a mother. How can she display herself like this? But she looks so free and so—he is almost driven to the word—so innocent, spraying the jet of water on her little boy, laughing with him, completely unaware that she is being watched; not at all like someone setting out to provoke lust.

Watching them, his mind leaps to Jane, and her questioning. Wouldn't he want to have a wife and a family of his own—a home of his own? He wonders why this memory comes back to him now.

With an effort he looks away and continues along the cracked, uneven footpath. The heat of the afternoon feels even more stifling. He looks around. There's nobody in sight. He slips out of the black jacket, pulls off the clerical collar and stuffs it roughly into a pocket, then unbuttons his shirt halfway down from the neck. The wind begins to feel almost pleasant as it starts to dry off some of the accumulated sweat. He slings the jacket over one shoulder and sets out on the last stage, stepping out with more vigour.

Several minutes later, with the church buildings coming into view, he hesitates, then stops. Out of his memory looms an image of the rector of the seminary: a lean man with a gaunt, pale face, jaws and chin strongly dark with black stubble, regardless of how recently and how thoroughly he has shaved. He is addressing the final-year group.

'Remember, gentlemen, a priest is and must always be a priest. Each of you will be a man set apart by God. You are called to strive towards saintliness. This must be visible in everything you do. You must never present yourselves like those who have chosen the temporal things of this world, which will pass away, rather than the eternal things of the world to come. Otherwise you will undermine the reverence due to God's Church.' The rector's eyes shine pale and hard behind his rimless glasses.

Under his imagined gaze Thomas buttons up his shirt and puts the collar and jacket back on. Near the far end of the block are the church buildings: first the convent, then the school, then the church itself, and finally the presbytery. By the time he reaches it he is running with sweat again.

The front door of the mean little box of a house is open. Thomas steps in from the narrow porch. In the sudden gloom of the narrow passage that runs straight through to the back of the house there seems to be a very odd shape: something like a pair of disembodied feet on the floor, with soles facing the doorway. He walks a few steps further, finally making out Father Kevin lying flat on his back on the floor of the passage, bare feet facing the front door.

'Ah, there you are, m'boy. I thought I could expect you soon. Have a good session with the witch doctor? It's been as hot as Hades in this little dog-box. I opened the place up to let a bit of air through but it's done me no good that I can feel. I was reading an article about the coldest air always being at the bottom. So I tried stretching out here on the lino. My God, boy, it was never like this in the Old Country.'

Slipping off his stifling jacket, Thomas looks down at the priest, who is wearing a grubby, sweat-stained ancient singlet above his usual black trousers, leaving its owner's puny arms and shoulders well displayed. The trousers are rumpled and dusty and the braces that usually hold them up are loose around his waist. Even allowing for the heat, Father Kevin makes a miserable sight.

Thomas quickly looks away.

'The wind might change soon. The easterly seems to be easing off. I'm going to have a cold shower; it's been a hot walk from the bus.' He steps past the small man and heads for the bathroom at the back of the house.

The first jet of cold water on his back and shoulders makes the young man gasp. But he adjusts to the shock and begins to enjoy the clean coolness as his skin gradually loses the memory of the sweat trickling down his back inside the sticky prison of his clerical clothes. He stands for ten minutes or so with the refreshing spray running over him until he feels restored and ready to face the rest of the afternoon.

Towelling himself dry, he looks at his reflection in the tarnished mirror on the back of the bathroom door. A sudden memory of the body of the young woman spraying her shrubs brings with it an equally sudden surge of excitement sweeping over him, and as it mounts, the inevitable wave of guilt follows.

He remembers the question that he was to take away from Macpherson for consideration: is it possible that he has been taught over years to surround anything sexual with an atmosphere of guilt? But if some pleasures are in fact sinful, as the church teaches, surely guilt is the right response to them. Macpherson, of course, doesn't use the word *sin*. But how would a man like that think about the idea? Perhaps he would argue that sin is not a reality. Could he think that it's just a useful fiction for making people feel guilty? Is it possible to think like this? Perhaps, for a non-believer. But where, then, is the basis for morality? And Macpherson doesn't appear to be an immoral person. The world of the non-believer is beyond Thomas's imagination. Life in general is becoming more complicated than he was led to believe, filling up with questions to which he finds no answers. He wraps a towel around his waist and heads for his own narrow bedroom that takes up the other back corner of the house.

At his doorway he pauses, aware of a voice at the front of the house. A female voice. A young woman is outlined against the bright glare outside the front door. With her in a stroller is a little girl with fat pink cheeks and fair hair peeping out from under a chequered sun bonnet that matches her chequered dress. He wonders how far the mother has pushed her through the afternoon heat.

Father Kevin is clambering to his feet in the passage. He pads barefoot towards the front door, pulling his braces up over his singlet as he goes.

'Wait a minute. I'm coming as fast as I can.' He sounds irritable.

Reaching the doorway, he looks the young woman up and down.

'I don't remember seeing you before,' he says abruptly. 'Are you a parishioner?'

She hesitates, looking down at the little girl for a moment, reaching down to touch her head. She seems nervous.

'No, I'm not.' She pauses for several seconds. 'In fact I'm not actually a Catholic.'

'Well, then.' The small man still sounds testy, possibly more so. 'What are you here for?'

She looks down at the little girl again and touches her head, as if she gets some support from the contact. Then she speaks, hesitantly at first, but more confidently as she gets underway.

'You see, I'm not a Catholic——'

Father Kevin interrupts impatiently. 'You've said that already.' He looks around quickly as if he's anxious to be rid of an annoyance.

'But I'm married to one.'

He grunts. 'Yes?'

'And when we married I promised to bring our children up as Catholics. And I really meant to do it. In fact I was thinking of becoming a Catholic myself. And my little girl here was baptised as one——'

'I don't see what problem you can have,' he cuts in. 'You made a promise: a solemn promise. You have an obligation to keep it. That is what promising means, isn't it?' His voice is blunt, challenging.

The young woman is silenced for a moment.

'Yes,' she says, and pauses. 'But I don't see how I can. Not how I can do it honestly.' She hurries on before he can interject. 'I've been reading a lot about the Catholic Church, and I can't accept, well, quite a number of things. But the main thing is the authority. A Catholic is supposed to accept the authority of the Church—the pope—isn't that right? And to believe whatever the teachings are? So, if the pope announced some new doctrine next week, I'd be expected to believe it.'

Father Kevin makes a snorting sound. 'What do you mean? What new doctrine are you talking about? There isn't anything of that sort as far as I know.'

'But if there was one,' she goes on hesitantly. 'I don't know what it would be. Popes have announced new doctrines before, haven't they? I was reading about the Assumption a few weeks ago. The cardinals voted on whether it should be made a compulsory belief, didn't they? And they weren't all in favour, according to the book I read. But the pope announced it all the same.'

Father Kevin makes an abrupt, dismissing gesture with one hand. He speaks with the same sharpness.

'The Assumption. You don't understand at all. That wasn't a new doctrine. Catholics believed it already. Most of them anyway.'

The young woman persists, though her voice is unsteady, with a tremble breaking in at times.

'But you don't understand what I'm talking about. What if I was there at that time? The week before the declaration I was free to believe it or not. That is, supposing I was a Catholic. Then the pope spoke, and from then on I was obliged to believe whatever he said. How can people believe something just because someone has told them to?'

The priest, outlined against the bright glare of the doorway, runs one hand across his bald head.

'Protestant thinking. Intellectual pride. A good Catholic accepts the wisdom of God, as revealed by his Holy Church through its clergy, and doesn't presume to think everything out for himself . . . or herself.'

Then he seems to sense his abrasiveness, and makes a new start, beginning with an effort to soften his voice and his approach.

'In our limited human understanding, we can't expect to fathom the mysteries of religion.' He looks around quickly, as if his heart is not really in this homily. 'Faith. That's the key. Faith and humility. And obedience. That's what you Protestants don't understand.' The confronting tone is back again. 'You must have been talking to your Protestant pastors.'

When she replies the tremble in her voice is more obvious, but she continues to defend herself.

'That's not true. I've been reading for myself. Thinking for myself. I did talk to an Anglican priest about it and he was very understanding. As far as he was concerned I made that promise under duress so I shouldn't feel bound by it. But he said that I should speak to you.'

Looking down the passage past Father Kevin's skinny right shoulder, Thomas can see that she is wiping her eyes with the back of her hand. The little girl, who has been sitting patiently in the stroller, is beginning to complain. The mother leans to pat her head.

'I'm not surprised,' the priest snaps. 'Mixed marriages never work. That's one thing we understood in the Old Country. We never trusted Protestants there. And we were right.' He turns, then swings back for a final shot. 'And another thing: Anglican ministers aren't priests. They don't have valid ordination.'

He turns his back on the young woman, pushing the door shut and closing off Thomas's view of her as she turns her back on the presbytery and makes her way down the narrow path to the street and the heat of the afternoon. He wonders how far she has to walk.

9

The Feast of Saint Francis Xavier

'Well, now. At last we've come to a saint I've heard about. I was beginning to think that I was totally uneducated in the matter of saints.' Macpherson rubs his cheek. He looks doubtful. 'At least his name is familiar. I remember being in a church that was named after him. I think it was for a funeral. And I've read about a school in Melbourne called Xavier College. A fairly expensive school, I believe. Exclusive. But what the man did, or what fate befell him—I'm rather vague about this. I've a faint memory about some connection with India, of all places, so I look forward to hearing more about him, and perhaps hearing about any memories that his story revives for you.' He sits back in his chair, eyes fixed on a spot on the wall above Thomas's head.

Thomas sinks back into the depths of his own chair, opens his book, and begins.

Among those who in the sixteenth century laboured most successfully in the conversion of nations, the most illustrious was Saint Francis Xavier, the Thaumaturgus of these latter ages, whom

Urban VIII justly styled the apostle of the Indies. This great saint was born in Navarre, at the castle of Xavier, eight leagues from Pampelona, in 1506. From his infancy he was of a complying, winning humour, and discovered a good genius and a propensity to learning.

His inclinations determined his parents to send him to Paris in the eighteenth year of his age where he entered the college of Saint Barbara, and commenced a course of scholastic philosophy. His faculties were hereby opened, and his penetration and judgment exceedingly improved; and the applause which he received agreeably flattered his vanity, which passion he was not aware of.

Saint Ignatius came to Paris in 1528, with a view to finish his studies, and after some time entered himself pensioner in the college of Saint Barbara. This holy man had conceived a desire of forming a society wholly devoted to the salvation of souls; and being taken with the qualifications of Peter Faber, called in French Le Fevre, a Savoyard, and Francis Xavier, who had been school-fellows, and still lived in the same college, endeavoured to gain their concurrence in this holy project. Xavier began to see into the emptiness of earthly greatness, and to find himself powerfully touched with the love of heavenly things. Yet it was not without many serious thoughts and grievous struggles that his soul was overcome by the power of those eternal truths. From Ignatius he learned that the first step in his conversion was to subdue his predominant passion, and that vain-glory was his most dangerous enemy. And well knowing that the interior victory over his own heart and its passions is not to be gained without mortifying the flesh and bringing the senses into subjection, he undertook this conquest by hair cloth, fasting, and other austerities.

When the time of the vacancy was come, in 1535, he performed Saint Ignatius' spiritual exercises; in which, such was his fervour, that he passed four days without taking any nourishment, and his mind was taken up day and night in the contemplation of heavenly things.

In 1534, on the feast of the Assumption of Our Lady, Saint Ignatius and his six companions, of whom Francis was one, had made a vow at Montmartre to visit the Holy Land and unite their labours for the conversion of the infidels. They travelled, in 1536, all through Germany on foot, loaded with their writings, in the midst of winter, which that year was very sharp and cold. Xavier, to overcome his passions, and punish himself for the vanity he had formerly taken in leaping (for he was very active, and had been fond of such corporal exercises) in the fervency of his soul, had tied his arms and thighs with little cords, which, by his travelling, swelled his thighs, and sunk so deep into the flesh as to be hardly visible.

The saint bore the pain with incredible patience, till he fainted on the road; and, not being able to go any farther, was obliged to discover the reason. His companions carried him to the next town, where the surgeon declared that no incision could be safely made deep enough, and that the evil was incurable. In this melancholy situation, Faber, Laynez, and the rest spent that night in prayer; and the next morning Xavier found the cords broken out of the flesh. The holy company joined in actions of thanksgiving to the Almighty, and cheerfully pursued their journey.

After waiting a whole year in Rome to find an opportunity of passing into Palestine, and finding execution of that design impracticable, on account of the war between the Venetians and the Turks, Saint Ignatius and his company offered themselves to his holiness, *to be employed as he should judge most expedient in the service of their neighbour. John III, King of Portugal, wrote to Don Pedro Mascaregnas, his ambassador in Rome, and ordered him to obtain six of these apostolic men, to be sent to plant the faith in the East Indies.*

Saint Ignatius could grant him only two, and pitched upon Simon Rodriguez, a Portuguese, and Nicholas Bobadilla, a Spaniard. The former went immediately by sea to Lisbon; Bobadilla, who waited to accompany the ambassador, fell sick, and by an over-ruling supernatural direction, Francis Xavier was substituted in his room, on the day before the ambassador began his journey.

The journey was performed all the way by land, over the Alps and Pyreneans, and took up more than three months. At Pampelona, the ambassador pressed the saint to go to the castle of Xavier, which was but a little distant from the road, to take leave of his mother, who was yet living, and of his other friends, whom he would probably never more see in this world. But the saint would by no means turn out of the road, saying, that he deferred the sight of his relations till he should visit them in heaven. This wonderful disengagement from the world exceedingly affected Mascaregnas, who by the saintly example and instructions of the holy man, was converted to a new course of life.

'Perhaps we could stop there. The story of Saint Francis Xavier is shaping like a rather long one, and promises to be a good deal longer; he's still well short of the Indies. I think we can interrupt it to find out whether any memories are coming to the surface.'

Thomas puts the book aside. He sits back, eyes closed, arms and legs relaxed, head resting against the back of the chair.

He recalls putting the book aside, a small ribbon-shaped leaf marking a page in the story of the life of Saint Francis Xavier. There is a clump of short twisted trees with narrow leaves, on a rocky headland. Under the sketchy foliage is a patch of mottled shade. He is sitting on the hard, uneven ground in this patch of shade. It is the middle of a blazing day. This is the only shelter from the sun as far as he can see in any direction; most of the headland is bare rock or low scrub only a foot or two high.

The patch of shade is barely enough for two people so although he has carefully placed the rucksack between him and Jane, she is still within arm's reach, lying on her back, eyes closed, apparently asleep. His gaze, as if it has a life and intentions of its own, strays over her body, registering the way her breasts push up under her once-white shirt, taking in the stains of mud and sweat on her clothes, noticing that her legs have relaxed slightly apart, and a fold of her skirt has slipped into the small space between them. An intense sense of her difference, her femaleness, is strangely mixed with a sharp perception of her vulnerability. He turns his head away and tries to focus his mind on their situation.

Before he took out *Lives of the Saints* they had been eating a couple of biscuits each and a handful of dried fruit and nuts, washing them down with swampy water they had found the previous morning. It had tasted of roots and decaying leaves and mud. Now they have less than one small bottle left between them and a long, hot afternoon ahead. Another day tomorrow, perhaps many more.

Between the stems of the stunted trees that are throwing this sketchy shade he scans the next stretch of the coast: another long sweep of beach, with swells breaking in white foam. A fine mist of spray hangs over the line along which the waves are crashing onto the sand. Behind the beach the dunes rise higher as they march inland, starkly white in the glare, with patches of low greyish vegetation here and there. At the far end, a long way off, there is a rocky promontory. How many more repetitions of this sequence of beach and headland must they trudge over, before seeing some sign of human habitation?

Thomas's mouth and throat feel as if they have been parched for days. He watches her for a few moments, her face half turned away from him, her breathing slow and steady. Carefully, he lifts the water bottle out of the pack, takes two or three extra mouthfuls, replaces the lid and returns the bottle quietly to the pack, thinking meanwhile, that this is only fair after all, when he is burdened with extra weight. She is relying on him to carry the food and water for both of them.

Minutes later she begins to stir, sits up with her back against the twisted stem of one of the small trees. She looks around and sees the book laid down on a slab of rock between them. After a few seconds of hesitation she speaks. May she look at it, just for a few minutes? She has noticed him deciding to carry it all this way, reading from it each day, and wondered.

Thomas feels the familiar prickly embarrassment about exposing himself to anyone outside the circle, but passes the book to her, wondering whether it will seem to her rather . . . odd. He goes back to scanning, or pretending to scan, the next stretch of beach and the rollers breaking on it. Out of the corner of his eye he sees her open the book where it is marked with the leaf, watching apprehensively as she looks over the double page she has opened and turns back to the beginning to read the story through. Little creases form in the middle of her forehead, just above her nose, giving her face an expression of serious concentration, with, at this moment, a suggestion of puzzlement.

She closes the book slowly and places it in her lap, staring into the distance at the beach and the line of spray hanging over it before turning towards him, hesitant. She can't understand the story she's just read. He takes the book from her outstretched hand without meeting her eyes, and replaces it in the pack. He was right to feel uncomfortable.

She makes another start. That bit about his mother. What's his name—Francis Xavier? About visiting his mother. Actually about not visiting his mother. She got the impression that he was supposed to be admired for that. Is that right? Admired for passing by without taking the trouble to visit his mother?

Thomas clears his dry throat and makes a start on an explanation. It's not just that, it's because he chose to do God's work instead. What God had called him to do—wanted him to do.

The young woman listens, creases still marking her forehead. It takes her some time to respond. What *did* God want him to do? Wouldn't God have wanted him to visit his mother? Especially if she was old and this was his last chance. Jane was brought up a Methodist, went to Methodist Sunday School. There were prizes for learning bible texts—Golden Texts, they called them—with attendance prizes too. What they learned at Sunday School was that God wanted them to be kind to people, especially old people, poor people, sick people, babies, children: anyone in need of kindness. Sometimes the teacher would organise them to take a little present that they had made, like a picture they'd drawn, to one of the old folk in the area. That was what they were taught: to do things like that.

To her way of thinking, this man Francis Xavier was being selfish, doing what he wanted to do without considering his mother; and imagining that God wanted him to do this, too. That's self-centred. What was the ambassador supposed to have learned from this example? Did he learn not to waste his time visiting his own elderly mother? As she saw it, he began with a better idea of the right thing to do. Maybe Francis needed to learn something from the ambassador.

The prickly feeling has spread from the back of Thomas's neck across his shoulders. He struggles to put an answer together. He begins an attempt: *there are some things more important than* . . . he pauses. His throat feels tight. Perhaps, in a way, now that he thinks about it, visiting his mother might have been the right thing to do. Without answering her he looks away, suddenly aware of the discomfort of sitting on the uneven stony ground. He grabs at the stem of one of the stunted trees to hoist himself up. Reaching for the rucksack, he stands, heaving it up onto his shoulders. They need to move on. They must find water soon; it's nearly all gone.

Jane stands too, levering herself up, rubbing her painful leg. They plod down the slope of the headland towards the next beach, Thomas trying to judge the distance to the next headland at the far end. And beyond that, how much further?

Two hours later they are still plodding through soft sand, and the next promontory still looks a good half hour away. Jane is lagging behind. When he looks back, she is limping more than in the morning. Perhaps he should have been more mindful of this and set an easier pace.

'Wait a bit, please, Thomas,' she calls to him.

He slows, stops, watches her struggling to catch up.

She flops down on the sand in front of him. She's so tired. She can't go on without a few minutes' rest at least. And she's so thirsty. Why don't they finish the last of the water? It'll run out some time very soon whatever they do.

He begins to object. Shouldn't they be pushing on, looking for more? Then thinks again. Why not? There's so little left. It won't take them much further anyway. He swings the pack down, pulls out the bottle, and hands it to her.

She holds the bottle to her mouth, takes three or four small careful mouthfuls, shakes it to gauge how much is left, and hands it back. There. She's had her share, nearly, anyway. He needs a bit more, carrying the extra weight for both of them.

Thomas feels as if something inside him is shrinking, tightening, as he remembers his secretive mouthfuls at the last stop. Has she picked up his thought, seen what he did. But she couldn't have done. She is offering him the bigger share freely, out of generosity.

He tips the bottle, tasting the muddiness of the last dregs, wondering where the next mouthful will come from.

Choosing a spot on the sand a few feet from her, Thomas flops down and watches the rollers crashing on the beach, enjoying the cool dampness as a slight onshore breeze drifts a cloud of fine spray over them.

★

They are trekking further along the beach towards the next headland, each step requiring as much mental as physical effort. He is walking ahead, trying to pick the firmest level of the sand. Sometimes it looks better high up above the wave line; sometimes it appears to be more firmly packed where the breakers have swept up the slope of the beach leaving it smooth and wet. Thomas keeps switching from one line to the other, but the change never makes much difference.

They are walking barefoot; shoes were discarded the previous day when they both found them a handicap in the soft beach sand. But that decision is turning out to be a mistake: his feet are beginning to blister. Occasionally he slows his stride and looks back to see how far she is lagging behind. Her feet are probably beginning to blister too; she hasn't complained about them, and he hasn't asked. Water bottles rattle in his pack at every stride, reminding him of their emptiness. His throat is parched and an ache at the back of his head has been slowly intensifying, but they must keep moving.

The next rocky headland is much closer, and on the near side of it he can make out something different from the lines of glaring white sand-hills with the occasional scatter of pale, greyish grass and low drab bushes: a small patch of deeper green in the face of the dunes.

As he trudges on the details gradually become clearer. The darker triangle is in the mouth of a small cleft in the dunes. On the far side the higher ground of the promontory rises, but he can't make out what is in the gap. Obviously there's a patch of vegetation quite different from what grows in the parched dunes and the thin dry soil of the rocky headlands. But what, and why?

At closer range he thinks he can pick out something else: a small gutter in the sand emerging from the mouth of the gully. Something there is shining in the sun, high up on the beach above the tide line, but the glare from the afternoon sun ahead makes it impossible to see the details. Despite his exhaustion, Thomas puts on a faster pace, anxiety gnawing at him.

From a few yards away it is clear that a small stream is trickling out of the mouth of a gully, spilling over a shelf of pale rock and flowing a few yards, before losing itself in the beach sand well above the level at which the waves are breaking and sweeping up the slope. Surely, he thinks, so close to the sea, it can't be fresh.

He drops to his knees without waiting to remove his pack and tries a mouthful cupped in his hand. Relief floods his mind. He turns and beckons, urgently.

'Fresh water! Thank God!'

He thinks of the miraculous spring that gushed out at the spot struck by the saint's staff in the story of Saint Sabas. Immediately another thought intrudes, unbidden, disrupting any idea of a miracle. This little stream was obviously here long before his arrival—here for decades by the look of the shrubbery around it. Why have conflicting thoughts like these recently been jostling for space in his mind more and more often?

★

The sand is cool against his back through his thin shirt. Thomas is lying in the dense shade cast by small deep-green trees growing in a narrow gap between the dunes. There is a faint sound of the water as it trickles down the stream bed and spills over the rock shelf at the edge of the beach. Outside the tent of leaves the glare on the beach is still harsh, but the sun is lower, dipping towards the sea to the west. He realises that he must have dropped off to sleep after drinking as much water as he could take. A few yards away Jane is still asleep, but beginning to stir.

She turns over muttering something, then abruptly sits up, rigid, looking around, eyes wide with alarm. As she turns far enough to see him watching her, the fear fades from her face. Settling back on one elbow, facing him, she explains her fright. It was a dream: she was swimming in a huge expanse of water with no shore in sight and nothing to suggest which way to swim to reach land. Then she woke suddenly and didn't know where she was. Until she saw him, and remembered.

Jane smiles momentarily at him and lies back on the cool, shaded sand, looking up into the canopy of leaves, speaking, as if to the leaves.

'What a godsend—this place, with the shade, and the coolness, and the water. Especially the water.'

Thomas, too, lies back on the sand looking up into the leaves, wondering about the meaning of that momentary smile. Was it a message of some sort for him? Or was it only relief at escaping from the dream? Her questions the previous day about his embarking on a celibate life—did they also have a meaning for him that he missed? He hadn't thought about this at the time and is sharply aware that this is, for him, uncharted territory. Wilderness.

Jane sits up again. Stands, her feet sinking into the loose sand of the side of the gully. She'll just go for a quick walk. Over this sand-hill. She'll be back in a couple of minutes.

After some initial confusion, Thomas has grasped the coded meaning. He'll do the same, over the hill on the other side of the gully. He tramps up the slope, with a backward glance at her heading in the opposite direction. Over the crest of the hill he changes direction, hurrying towards the head of the gully. Dropping to his hands and knees, he creeps cautiously to a vantage point from which, through a screen of coarse grey grass, he can peer in the direction she has taken. And there she is, glancing around quickly so as to make sure that she is out of sight. Apparently satisfied, she hitches up her skirt, pulls down her pants and squats.

Thomas is rigid with anxiety and guilt about being seen himself but continues to stare at something he has only imagined, shamefully, in the vaguest way. Excitement about seeing and anxiety about being seen—the two feelings compete for space in his consciousness.

She stands, pulls up her pants and smooths down her skirt. The unselfconscious innocence of her movements suddenly turns Thomas's attention onto himself. What is he doing, peering at her furtively, in hiding? He feels shamed, sullied. He cringes down behind the grass screen, backing away from his vantage point, on hands and knees, taking to his feet only when he feels safer, hurrying to be back in position in time, or at least to be returning to the mouth of the gully from the appropriate direction.

He is back where the stream spills onto the beach when she pushes through the shrubs on the other slope. He watches her feet sliding and sinking in the sand, and feels, as he tries to look her in the face, another level of shame. As if he has sullied her as well as himself. And yet, what harm has he done her? If she doesn't know?

Macpherson has listened without comment. Thomas now waits for a response, wondering what the older man has been thinking about his revelations. Perhaps it was a mistake to reveal so much. He has never exposed himself like this before except in a confession to a priest. But this man, as he said at the outset, passes no judgment, does not even appear to think it. How can this be, that he makes no comment on these memories, except to express satisfaction that the recovery strategy is working so well?

Macpherson finally speaks.

'There is a good deal in today's memories for us to think about. Both of us. We will return to some of them on a later occasion but for now, let me ask you about your dreams. Is there a dream from this last week that you can describe for me?'

Thomas is relieved to move into less intimate territory.

'I had one the night before last. This is quite strange: it's rather like Jane's nightmare, being in a huge expanse of water, with no sense of direction. Do you think that means something important? The similarity?'

'Well now, as I've said before, that's hard for me to say. It may be telling you something. You're the dreamer, not me. But perhaps you should describe it to me.'

'I'm floating in the water. It seems to be late in the afternoon, or evening, really, but I don't have any idea how I got there. The sun has set and the light is beginning to fade. I look around and see that there's a shore behind me, not very far, maybe a hundred yards away. It's not a long swim but while I'm looking at the shore I realise that I'm drifting away from it. It doesn't feel like being caught in a current. It's as if the whole mass of water is moving steadily away from the land, and me with it. I'm a fair swimmer, but somehow

I know in my dream that there's no point in trying to swim against this drift.

'So I turn around to see where I'm being carried, and in front of me, and from side to side, there's an open expanse of water, quite smooth, and moving as a body gently in the same direction. At first I can't see any sign of land; the water seems to go on forever. But then I think I can make something out. It's away on the horizon in the direction I'm moving: just a low shape that's outlined against the last of the light. I can't pick out any detail there.

'And that seems to be the end of the dream, at least as far as I can remember.'

Macpherson has been sitting back in his chair, face tilted up towards the ceiling, listening intently. He brings his head forward to focus on the younger man.

'Well now, a very interesting dream. And how did you feel about this situation? Drifting away from land into a wide expanse of water. It could be frightening, or possibly exciting, or . . .'

Thomas considers for a few minutes.

'Frightening? No, I don't think I found it frightening. Not particularly exciting either. As far as I remember I felt fairly calm about it. But I was . . . puzzled, maybe that's the word. Or perhaps a little insecure. I just had no idea what was in store for me—what was coming.'

'That's very interesting. This may be a very profitable dream for you to spend some time with. I suggest that you put some thought into the difference between this dream and the one you told me about two weeks ago: the dream about drifting down a channel between two steep high banks. What are these two dreams saying to you about what is going on under the surface of your mind?

★

Thomas settles, as far as possible, on the hard seat of the bus shelter. He has a substantial wait for the next bus back toward the parish. He thinks about Macpherson's suggestion that there might be ideas brewing somewhere down under the surface of his mind. Could he have meant new thoughts about the shape of his life? But surely he understands that the shape of Thomas's life is already set—has been for years.

Without any warning his mind is taken over by an image of the young woman with the little boy and the small house with the red door. He wonders whether he will see her again, remembers watching her play with her toddler and being struck with a sense of her innocence. Innocence in spite of her bikini, which the archbishop had declared to be a threat to the sanctity of family life.

The thought occurs to him that it must have been a few decades since the archbishop had any experience of family life. And Thomas himself: for the last nine years his contact with family life has been scanty. For both of them the long-past experience had been a child's experience. What would they know about family life from an adult point of view? He thinks of innocence. Perhaps it is to be found in places where he would not have looked for it until recently.

Thomas looks around for a distraction from these unsettling thoughts. Of course. He picks up *Lives of the Saints* and opens it at random, finding himself facing, on the second of January, a saint he has never encountered before: Saint Macarius the

Younger who, like many another early Christian saint, lived as a hermit in the Syrian or Palestinian desert.

The story is about exploits of extreme austerity, for which the man was widely renowned. One day he inadvertently killed a gnat that was biting him and immediately regretted losing the opportunity to suffer the pain in full. So he hurried to a marshy area infested with savage stinging flies and endured them for six months, returning unrecognisably disfigured by sores and swellings.

Subsequently, it seems, someone suggested to Macarius that he leave the desert and go to Rome to serve the sick in hospitals there. After some thought the saint rejected this as a temptation from the devil to seek attention and esteem, instead remaining in the desert to devote himself to further conspicuous extremes of self-mortification.

Where is the edification to be distilled from this story? Thomas finds himself, almost unwillingly, wondering what Macpherson would have to say about the life of Macarius the Younger. It is not hard to imagine. And what could he himself say in response to explain the virtue displayed in this man. What *is* the virtue? Is this innocence? Why is it that he can't find the inspiration that he usually finds in *Lives of the Saints*? This story has him facing another set of disturbing questions.

The sound of an engine cuts across the path of his thoughts. The bus is at the end of the street. Glad for the distraction, he shuts the book and stands.

10

A Moral Lesson

Father Kevin looks up from the racing pages.

'There it is. Dinner. Not before time, either. You open the door, m'boy. I wonder what horrors await us tonight.'

A tall thin nun stands outside; a dark silhouette against the light from the early evening sky. She holds the usual tin tray carrying two dinner plates, the contents hidden by battered aluminium covers, and two dessert dishes with something inside that is hard to identify in the fading light. Her thin lips are shut in a straight line across her narrow face. Her eyes are dark behind the small-lensed, steel-rimmed glasses. She does not look happy.

'Sister Agatha. Please come in.' He stands aside for her to pass, feeling awkward, pressing his back against the open door to avoid any danger of contact. The nun nods, looking him momentarily in the face, and stalks up the passage. Her long black habit swishes as she goes.

The older man is already sitting at the table with the red Laminex top and chrome legs. Sister Agatha puts the tray down a little more noisily, Thomas thinks, than is strictly necessary.

Barely glancing at her, Father Kevin intones a 'Thank you, Sister,' without obvious enthusiasm. The tall nun nods, looks at the priest without any change in her expression and, without a word, turns to head back down the passage. The swishing of her dead-black habit is the only sound; her feet seem completely silent on the floor. Thomas follows to see her out and returns to the table.

The priest peers at him with his usual half-grin.

'A peculiar one, that. Sour. It's a good thing she's in the convent. Some lucky man was saved from the fate of holy matrimony with her. Now what's she brought us today? Jelly and custard for sweets. What a surprise! I reckon we get it four times a week. No, let's be fair, maybe only three times a week. Do you think they water down the milk when they make this custard? It always looks a bit transparent to me. And what about the first course?'

He tips off one of the dented aluminium covers.

'There it is: another culinary classic from the convent kitchen. I wonder what they do to these chops to make the fat so thick and greasy. The skill probably comes with their training. And mashed potato. I hate mashed potato, you know. They know it too.' He prods with his fork into the whitish-grey mass and encounters resistance. 'A lump. I should have said partly mashed potato. And just feel it, m'boy. Dead cold. Near enough to it anyway. Why do you reckon they built the convent and the presbytery at opposite ends of the property? One fellow thought it was to preserve Sister Agatha's virtue. I reckon it's to give the nuns plenty of time to let hot food get cold while they bring it across from the kitchen.

'Mind you, that Agatha, she'd find a way to get it here cold regardless of how close we were. A couple of times lately I've seen her at it: putting the tray down and kneeling in front of the statue of Our Lady in the grotto out there. Over ten minutes she stayed there once—I timed her—and the meal getting colder every second. Savoury mince I think it was that time. Unsavoury mince would have been a bit nearer to the mark. Bloody ingenious, you have to admit. She knows I can see the grotto from the front window, but I can hardly complain about it, can I? She's overcome by pious fervour. Feels inspired to fire off a few Hail Marys as she passes. How can anyone argue with that? I tell you, boy, she's cunning. I reckon she feels hostile about having to feed us. Probably thinks she deserves better. So she makes us suffer for it, one way or another.

'I tell you what, let's have a whisky. Drown our sorrows. Christen them, anyway. Here we are, Vat 69. The pope's licence plate number. Courtesy of a grateful parishioner. I gave him the moral guidance he was hoping for about his tax return. Can't afford to buy the stuff m'self. It's a long time between little luxuries here, m'boy.' Father Kevin grins on one side of his narrow face, holding out the Vegemite glass with the smaller ration of whisky.

'And another thing, while I'm thinking about Sister Agatha. How would you like to take a Religious Knowledge lesson for me at the school? Agatha's class. You might as well start to get your hand in. I'll be off at the bank talking about a loan for a new car. Ten o'clock, the lesson is. Half an hour or so.

Thomas takes a small tentative sip. Whisky. His first experience with it. Perhaps it's an acquired taste.

'I suppose so, but what's the lesson going to be about? And what sort of class? How old are they?'

Father Kevin considers.

'The fifth standard. That's Agatha's class. I suppose they'd be about ten, wouldn't they? All girls of course. The boys are off to the Brothers' a couple of years earlier. And what's it about? I'll have to think a bit.'

He takes a mouthful from his Vegemite glass and sighs, looking up at the ceiling.

'Vat 69. Good stuff. I wonder whether they have it in heaven. Or hell, for that matter.' He grins, pours himself another half-inch, and looks dubiously at Thomas, with the bottle poised. 'I don't suppose you fancy another?'

Thomas shakes his head, and takes a small uncertain sip.

'Very wise, at your age. Start gradually. The Ten Commandments. That's what I was doing with the class. One a week. I can't remember where we'd got to. Thou shalt not kill; maybe that's the one. Or did we do that last week? They'll tell you anyway. It should be easy enough, you just talk a bit, ask a few questions, enquire whether they have any questions for you. You know the sort of thing.'

The small man reaches for his glass, swallows the contents in one gulp, grimaces, then sighs.

'Now. Let's find out whether we've worked up enough courage to face that partly mashed potato.'

★

Thomas walks down the wide school corridor. It's another muggy day. Beads of perspiration gather across his brow and upper lip and he feels the sweat gathering inside his unforgiving clerical garb. Sister Agatha's room, number four, is the last on the right. He peers through the glass panel in the door. It's a very quiet, orderly class; the girls are all at their desks copying something into their exercise books. They look up from time to time to where the blackboard must be, some of them with puzzled expressions, then return to the task. He can't see what they are copying.

The nun is standing tall above one small girl. A long finger is pointing to something the girl has just written. A sharp penetrating voice with an Irish edge is clearly audible on Thomas's side of the door.

'Look at that word, Brigid Ryan. Now look at the word I wrote on the board. Are they the same?'

Brigid looks up towards the blackboard. She seems to be mystified. Her eyes move between the board and her exercise book several times. The two plaits at the back of her head bob up and down, then a small light seems to dawn. She shakes her head slowly, the plaits swing from side to side.

'I asked you a question, Brigid Ryan. Are they the same or different?'

'Different, Sister.' The small voice barely reaches Thomas on the other side of the door. The small face is turned down towards the floor, a deep blush creeping up to it from her neck.

'And how are they supposed to be?' There is another pause while the girl sits looking with a puzzled expression between desk and blackboard. 'Well, girl, are they supposed to be different? Or the same?'

Brigid manages at last to pick up the hint.

'The same, Sister.' She blurts it out eagerly, as an important discovery.

'So what do you do about it?'

The mumbled reply can't be heard outside, but Thomas can see the small hand scrubbing away at the page with a rubber.

'I don't know, Brigid Ryan, how to get some sense into your thick head.' The nun's bony knuckles are knocking on the top of the small girl's head who flinches with each knock, her plaits bobbing up and down.

Thomas interrupts with the knocking of his knuckles on the door. Sister Agatha looks up sharply and sweeps across to open the door.

'Mr Riordan. This is a surprise. Is Father Kevin ill?' Her mouth shuts straight and tight.

Thomas does not get the impression that the surprise is a pleasant one.

'No, he's quite well. He had some business to attend to for the parish. He asked me to stand in for him.'

He glances up at the blackboard. There it is, the text that little Brigid Ryan and the others have been trying so earnestly to copy: *Ireland, land of saints, scholars and shamrocks.* He turns back to the nun.

'Father Kevin asked me to take his place for this Religious Knowledge class.'

Sister Agatha purses her thin lips. She looks dubious.

'I see.'

'He told me it was about the Commandments, about one of them really, but he couldn't remember which one.'

At this the nun smiles the faintest of smiles. It curves her mouth almost imperceptibly, but doesn't seem to reach her eyes.

'I see.'

Thomas is floundering. She is not trying to make this easy.

'Perhaps you can help me, Sister. Which of the Commandments is it for this week?'

She smiles faintly again. Pauses for a moment. Then delivers the blow.

'"Thou shalt not commit adultery."' She pauses again to let the frightening information sink in. 'I shall just go to the back of the room to mark some spelling tests. They are all yours, Mr Riordan.'

Thomas walks to the front of the classroom. He stumbles on the single step up to the level of the teacher's desk, but manages to avoid sprawling on the floor. Something in his belly seems to be tied in a knot. What in God's name is he going to say about adultery?

He looks around the room. At least forty-five ten-year-old girls. Probably fifty. All those plaits and snub noses. And all those freckles. Amazing, the number of them with freckles and ginger hair, their eyes trained unblinkingly on him.

He starts on safe neutral territory.

'Good morning, girls.'

A drawn-out period of scraping and clattering follows as the girls, surely there must be at least fifty of them, maybe nearer to sixty, struggle to their feet. Then a ragged sing-song chorus: 'Good morning, Father.'

His right hand goes up to fiddle with his collar. A nervous habit, he knows. He must try to control it.

'No, girls, I'm not a Father. My name is Mister Riordan.'

Another ragged, sing-song chorus: 'Good morning Mister Riordan.' A momentary giggle comes out of the middle of the group. He can't pick out the giggler.

'Thank you, girls. Now sit down please.'

Another extended period of scraping and clattering follows as the girls settle into their seats. Thomas briefly entertains the desperate thought that if he told the class to stand and sit twelve or fifteen times, that would go close to filling the half-hour, and he could completely avoid the terrifying prospect of explaining adultery to fifty ten-year-old girls. Or more.

He glances to the back of the room. Sister Agatha is sitting at a spare desk, a stack of papers in front of her, pencil in hand. She crosses out a word on the top page with a forceful stroke. He tries to make a start of some sort.

'Now, girls, who remembers which of the Commandments we are going to talk about this week?'

There is a period of silence that feels like a full ten seconds. All those eyes are wide open and focused on him. He clears his throat. His hand moves nervously up towards his collar, but he manages for once to head it off. He runs his fingers through his hair instead. There is another giggle from somewhere in the middle of the room. Then Sister Agatha's sharp voice from the back: 'Brigid Ryan. Stop that stupid giggling, girl'.

Thomas knows he must do something to take control of the situation. But what? He begins, 'Well girls, the Commandment for today is: *Thou shalt not commit adultery*'.

Another period of silence follows. He continues: 'Does anyone know what . . .' The question dies in his throat. What if one of the girls answers? What would she say? And how would he handle the situation then? He racks his brains. A fragment comes to mind from one of the books in the seminary library: *This Commandment forbids fornication and all wilful pleasure in the irregular motions of the flesh*. Would this be helpful? It would surely make the situation a great deal worse. He remains paralysed.

Eventually a small hand is raised: perhaps a saving distraction. He points to the hand-raiser. 'Yes?' She struggles to her feet. There is a remarkable amount of clattering of furniture for one small person.

'Please, Father.'

'Mister. My name is Mister Riordan.'

'Please Mister Riordan, what is adultery?'

Thomas's mouth opens but no sound emerges. Even if he could find a way to broach the subject, his knowledge of what is involved is rudimentary. His mouth opens and shuts a couple of times. His fingers are inside his collar again.

At the back of the room Sister Agatha is standing. She has stood without a sound. She speaks.

'Thank you, Mr Riordan. That will do for now.'

She is moving forward down the centre aisle. She moves silently. Around her mouth is the tightest of tight smiles.

'I can take over for the rest of the lesson.'

Thomas understands. He has been tried in the balance and found wanting. His mouth opens and shuts once more. He nods, backs towards the door, collides with the front desk in the first row, turns, opens the door, and at last makes his escape.

Safely outside, he pauses in the wide corridor. Sister Agatha's voice is audible through the closed door. She is explaining adultery to the class. It is, she explains, a particularly grave sin. It is a sin that destroys bodies as well as souls. That is all the girls need to know about adultery at this stage. It is a sin that only adults can commit. As they might have guessed from its name.

She moves on briskly to the results of the spelling test she has just marked, and the consequences of those results for the girls who have failed to meet expectations. Thomas thinks he hears Brigid Ryan's name mentioned as he retreats down the corridor towards the safety of the outside world.

11

The Feast of Saint Peter Chrysologus

Thomas sits back in his chair. He feels relaxed without needing to work on relaxation. This routine is coming more easily to him. With a nod from Macpherson he finds his page: December 4, the Feast of Saint Peter Chrysologus, Archbishop of Ravenna, A.D. 450. He launches into the story.

Saint Peter was a native of Imola, anciently called Forum Cornelii, a town in the ecclesiastical state, near Ravenna. He was taught the sacred sciences, and ordained deacon, by Cornelius, bishop of that city, of whom he always speaks with veneration, and the utmost gratitude. He calls him his father, and tells us, that in his whole conduct all virtues shone forth, and that by the bright lustre of his actions he was known to the whole world.

Under his prudent direction our saint was formed to perfect virtue from his youth by the exercises of an interior life, and understood that to command his passions and govern himself was true greatness, and the only means to learning to put on the spirit of Christ. The more easily to accomplish this great and arduous work of subduing and regulating his passions, and forming the spirit of

Christ in his soul, he embraced a monastic state, and had served God in it with great fervour and simplicity for some time, when he was placed in the archiepiscopal see of Ravenna.

The archbishop John dying about the year 430, the clergy of that church, with the people, chose a successor, and entreated the bishop of Imola to go at the head of their deputies to Rome, to obtain the confirmation of Pope Sixtus III. Cornelius took with him his deacon Peter, and the pope (who, according to the historian of Ravenna, had been commanded to do so by a vision the foregoing night) refused to ratify the election already made, and proposed Peter as the person designed by heaven for that post; in which, after some opposition, the deputies acquiesced.

Our saint, after receiving the episcopal consecration, was conducted to Ravenna, and there received, with extraordinary joy, the emperor Valentinian III and his mother, Galla Placidia, then residing in that city. The holy bishop extenuated his body by fasting, and offered his tears to God for the sins of his people, whom he never ceased to teach no less by example than by words. When he entered on his charge, he found large remains of pagan superstition in his diocese, and several abuses had crept in among the faithful in several parts; but the total extirpation of the former, and the reformation of the latter, were the fruit of the holy pastor's zealous labours.

Among the remains of heathenish superstition, which he laboured to extirpate, he reckons the riotous manner of celebrating the New Year's day; of which he says, 'He who will divert himself with the devil, can never reign with Christ.' It appears that he often preached in the presence of the emperor, and of the catholic empress Placidia, mother of three children, Valentinian III, Placidia, and Eudocia.

In 448, our saint received Saint Germanus of Auxerre with great honour at Ravenna, and, after his death, esteemed it no small happiness to inherit his cowl and hair shirt. He did not long survive: for, in 452, when Attila approached Ravenna, John, Saint Peter's successor, held his see, and went out to meet him. The saint being forewarned of his approaching death, returned to Imola, his own country, and there gave to the church of Saint Cassian, a golden crown set with jewels, a gold cup, and a silver paten, preserved to this day with great reverence. Peter died at Imola, probably on the 2nd of December, 450, and was buried there in Saint Cassian's church. The greatest part of his relics are preserved there; but one arm is kept in a rich case at Ravenna.

Macpherson's gaze shifts down from the ceiling to Thomas's face.

'Well, now. A story with its own interest. Less striking, perhaps, than the previous two. There are some details that we might pursue later. But for now, first things first. You closed the book on that story a few weeks ago. Go back to that time. See it as happening now. Where are you? What are you doing?'

Thomas closes the book, puts it down on the wide, leather-covered arm of his chair. He shuts his eyes. Behind his shut eyelids he sees himself closing the book, putting it down on sand. On the sand of a beach. It's a long beach, backed, like all the beaches, by sand-hills, throwing back at him a harsh white midday glare.

A hot wind is blowing off the land, carrying with it the scent of many miles of bush baking in the sun, and for Thomas a strange sense of foreboding. Huge waves are breaking on the beach in a flurry of foam. As each of them peaks and begins to turn over, the wind whips spray off its crest and blows it seaward.

The shore is steep, sloping down into deep water a short distance out. The waves are rolling in at an angle, and each one crashes down and sweeps diagonally up the slope. Then a powerful back-surge washes down and under the foot of the next. Thomas watches the backwash from a massive breaker being sucked out and down into deeper water as its successor curls over it.

He turns towards his rucksack to stow *Lives of the Saints* inside. Beyond it, a few yards away, Jane is resting, lying back on the sand, turned towards him. Her face is red and rough from sunburn. Skin is peeling from her nose and her forehead and her cheeks, and from her arms below her short-sleeved shirt. She is not dressed for this much exposure. There are beads of sweat on her face and her clothes are stained. It has been a difficult morning, trudging along this endless beach with a searing north-easterly breeze promising no relief.

They move on, making slower progress on blistered feet. She is walking quite close beside him, but this no longer sets off the tension in his shoulders and his neck that he felt on earlier days.

After half an hour of silence she speaks. *This beach and the dunes behind it seem to go on forever. Not a leaf of shade anywhere.* Could they stop for a while and swim, to cool off and to get a bit cleaner?

They stop and stand, looking at the steep slope and the towering swells crashing down on it. He points to the under-tow sucking back under every breaking wave into deep water only a few yards out. He doesn't think that it looks safe. How good a swimmer is she?

She takes a few steps down the slope and stands, letting the next breaker sweep up over her feet and ankles, and up to her knees. The backwash drags hard at her legs down towards the base of the next wave. She retreats up the slope to dry sand above the wave line, hurrying, looking anxiously over her shoulder at the much bigger swell crashing down close behind her. She turns to him. He's right; the sea is not safe here. They go back to trudging through the loose dry sand, sweating in the wind that feels as if it is blowing out of an oven.

Time passes. The two are still making their slow and painful way along the same beach, the sun still high in the sky beating relentlessly down on them. They are approaching the end of the sandy shore line. Two or three hundred yards ahead it is replaced by a ledge of black rock a foot or so above the level of the sea. A parallel shelf of the same rock forms a reef forty or fifty yards out from the shore, with huge swells breaking, throwing up spouts of spray, spilling white wash into the strip of sheltered water between the two lines of rock. A broad streak of white foam runs along the centre of the channel, but closer to shore the surface is smoother and the water transparent.

They stand at the edge of the rock shelf, looking down several feet to a sandy bottom with dark patches here and there. Tufts of green seaweed bright as lettuce grow out of the rock, and small striped yellow and black fish dart around.

She looks up at him, pausing for a moment, as if she has to build up her confidence for what she has to say. This is the place. She must get into the water here to clean up. She feels dirty—filthy. Running with perspiration. And these clothes—she's had them on for far too long. It must be three days since they left the other pack behind with the spare clothes. She has to wash them here as well as she can. Would he mind? Going back into the sand-hills, while she tries to get clean?

Thomas remembers staring at her for a few seconds, before understanding dawns. Of course, yes, and perhaps later, he can do the same.

He places the rucksack onto the rocks and turns his back on the ocean, heading inland, up a gully between two steep dunes. When he looks back two or three times she is still standing, facing in his direction.

Turning out of the gully, he loses sight of her but after a few moments' hesitation he begins scrambling up the steep slope of the first dune, using his hands in the dry sand as well as his blistered feet. He's panting, and only in part from the exertion. A mounting excitement is taking him over as he works his way up to the crest, which is crowned in one place by a clump of coarse grey coastal vegetation. He finds a vantage point where, lying flat on the sand, he can raise his head and peer through the sparse stems and leaves.

The huge expanse of ocean, darker in the distance, with lines and flecks of white crawling across the surface, is punctuated closer to the shore by those massive swells. He identifies the dark rock of the shoreline and finds Jane. She has her back to him, but twists round at that moment, scanning the dunes. She turns away again and sits on the rock ledge, her feet in the water at the edge of the channel.

Her hands are busy at the front of her shirt. Glancing quickly around, she slips it off, revealing her upper arms and back, and brassiere. He realises that he's not sure how the word is pronounced. He has seen one only a few times on dummy figures in shop window displays. The sight was disturbing. But here is one on a living, moving woman. Even from the back at some distance, it is exciting. He is panting even faster than he was while scrambling up the steep face of the dune, and his pulse is thumping against the sand. He can feel the hair standing up on the back of his neck.

She leans forward, rinsing her shirt in the sea, rubbing it between her hands, swirling it from side to side, lifting it up for inspection several times before she is satisfied. She half turns to lay it on the rock behind her, quickly scanning the dunes at the same time, no doubt to reassure herself of her privacy in the huge, exposed landscape.

Her hands are busy behind her back at the fastenings, and she slips the brassiere off her shoulders. Thomas thinks he catches a momentary glimpse of the beginning of the curve of one breast. She leans forward and goes through the washing movements with this garment: the rubbing, swirling, rinsing.

Then she half turns again to lay it out on the rock behind her. Thomas gets a clearer view of her left breast as she turns her head, looking up into the dunes, where he is sure he is out of sight behind his screen.

Jane pauses for a few moments, as if hesitating, unsure what to do next. Then she slips forward into the edge of the channel, standing with her back to the rocky shelf and hidden by it up to above her waist. He watches intently, with a tight feeling in his belly, as she leans forward, swaying from one foot to the other. She is stepping out of her skirt, once a crisp blue and white, now stained with mud and sweat. It appears on the surface as she swirls it around, scrubs and swirls again and again. Then the skirt too is flung behind her onto the rock of the shore.

Thomas is suddenly aware that he is holding his breath as he watches her next movements. Again she is bending forward and swaying from one foot to the other. She is stepping out of her pants. Although she is largely out of sight behind the ledge of rock, he is intensely aware that she must be standing in the clear water, totally naked. The thought of her nakedness is overwhelming. His excitement reaches a level that can't be resisted. He turns on his side, unfastens belt and buttons, and begins, slowly, not wanting to hurry the peaking of the wave of his pleasure, to enjoy her from his place of hiding.

He watches as she scrubs and swirls and rinses this last garment. She works on it for some time. Then she turns fully around to toss it, thoroughly scrubbed and rinsed, onto the shore, and Thomas finally sees both her breasts. Even at this distance the darker pink nipples stand out against the fairness of the surrounding skin. Then she turns away and they are gone.

She stands there, apparently undecided, for perhaps half a minute. Then she plunges forward, swimming towards the deeper water of the middle of the channel. Buttocks and thighs flash into view, breaking the surface of the water, and the wave of pleasure breaks and washes irresistibly over him.

The surge recedes and the backwash sucks him down, as always, into black guilt. He looks away from her, slides back from the crest of the dune, lies on his back on the slope. Asking himself, as always, why he did it. Why did he put himself in the way of temptation? Why did he start? Why did he let himself go on?

He can't say how long he lies there, feeling a dark emptiness in his belly. It might be as long as ten minutes before he realises that perhaps he should head back to the shore, or at least find out whether the time is right.

12

The Last Wave

Sliding up to the peak of the dune again Thomas locates her clothes near his pack on the rock ledge. It's only when he scans the shoreline some distance to the right of where she entered the water that he picks Jane out in the middle of the channel.

She is swimming, what looks like a strong, competent breast-stroke, apparently heading towards where her clothes lie on the rock. But she appears to be moving backwards, not fast, but steadily, in the opposite direction, towards the far end of the channel. He watches her for a minute or two but fails to make any sense of what he is seeing.

Standing on the ridge looking right and left along the shoreline, suddenly he sees. The breakers and the backwash are sweeping into the left-hand end of the channel. The wash is spilling over the outer reef. The band of foam moving on the surface betrays the build-up of a current, a rip, steadily deepening and strengthening, sweeping along the channel from left to right. And where then? At the far end he can make out a gap in the outer reef, with some rocks jutting through the surface, and the rip surging against them, through the gap and out through the breakers to the open sea, the ocean.

Thomas starts down the seaward slope of the dune, plunging, taking great strides, sliding awkwardly in the soft sand. At much the same time Jane seems to realise her danger. He sees her turn and try to swim across the current towards the outer reef. He sees her lunge for a handhold on the edge of the rock shelf, then losing her grip and being swept further along, grasping for other handholds, losing them, calling for help.

Thomas reaches the shoreline. Opposite him on the other side of the channel Jane has managed to get a grip on a projecting rib of rock. But the current, stronger here, is surging and swirling around her, dragging at her. She is struggling to keep her handhold against the force of it. She turns her head, sees him, calls with shrill terror in her voice. *Please, Thomas. I can't hold on for long.*

He stands on the rock ledge, hesitating. For a few moments he feels paralysed, body and mind, a circuit of conflicting thoughts and emotions churning through him. He will swim out to her. Together they might be able to . . . But what if they are both swept out?

He plunges into the waist-deep water at the edge of the channel. Instantly the force of the current is dragging at him, even here, standing well clear of its full power. Could he get to her safely across the middle of the rip? And if he did, what would they do then? The outer reef gives no safety, with the heavy surf breaking over it. He tries swimming a few strokes towards her but with every stroke he loses more control to the surges pulling him away, and he is still well short of the centre of the channel where the current is strongest. Thomas looks towards the gap in the reef and the jagged rocks with foam driven over and around them by the force of the water sweeping out towards the breaking waves, and is gripped by the terrifying image of himself being swept out over those jagged rocks. He turns while he can, and swims quickly back to the safety of the edge.

Another frightening thought swoops into his consciousness like a bird of prey. He has just, up in the dunes, been guilty of a grave sin. A man who dies with a grave sin on his soul has no hope of escape from hell. Images of eternal flames and souls writhing in everlasting torment come to him from countless books and sermons. What can he do? He backs against the rock wall of the channel for support, overcome again by agonising indecision, looking desperately around for some other way of helping her, but knowing under his desperation that there is no other way.

Suddenly she loses her grip. The surging rip takes control, pulling her towards the end of the channel. She struggles hard against the current all the way, clutching desperately at jagged rocks jutting above the water as she is swept against them. Although she manages to get a handhold on several of them for a short time, she is dragged away. Thomas hears her calling to him for help, screaming. Yet he stands rigid, in helpless horror.

He sees her swept out into the breakers beyond the gap in the outer reef. An immense wave breaks over her, and she disappears for what seems a long time. Then her head reappears in the face of another massive swell. Jane is looking towards him, floundering, struggling, one arm waving. And her voice, harsh, rising to a high pitch of terror. *Please. Help me, Thomas.*

Then the last wave breaks over her, and he does not hear her voice again.

For a long time Thomas stands, immobilised, backed hard against the security of the rock wall. Every joint in his body seems to be locked in position. His mind, too, seems locked, fixed on the image of a huge wave frozen in the instant before breaking, and her head in the face of it.

Finally he climbs onto the dark rock ledge of the shore and paces one way and the other along it, scanning the churning sea beyond the reef, desperately, as if this, somehow, might bring her back into view. But she is certainly gone. And he had stood there, watching, wavering, doing nothing.

For a moment Thomas glimpses himself as if through her eyes, as she struggled in the face of that last wave breaking over her. He imagines what must have gone through her mind in that moment, crying out to him, looking toward him standing helplessly, the instant before she was overwhelmed. His throat chokes with a soundless wail struggling to emerge,

He collapses to his knees and tries to address a plea for help to God who must surely be present in some way, watching perhaps from above the harsh blue of the sky, but realises that he doesn't know what he is praying for. Help for her, or for himself? And what sort of help? Is he pleading for her to appear miraculously, perhaps from behind him, wearing the blue-and-white skirt and white blouse now so familiar, with the stains of sweat and mud washed away? He knows such things do not happen outside the lives of the saints. Is he pleading for time to be turned back so that he can have another chance while she is still alive, while that last wave has not yet broken, to do something? But he knows with the same certainty that time always moves onward. Some opportunities to act come only once, and he did not grasp this one. Now there is nothing to be done.

Images flood his consciousness. Jane's face, surrounded by the foam of a breaking wave, her eyes wide with terror. The face glimpsed briefly in the plane window, engulfed in flames, distorted by agony. Both mouths open, screaming for deliverance. The faces swirl around in his mind, replacing each other, then merging and combining into a single blurred image of horror, projecting a single despairing wail to the heavens. Thomas's own mouth, he realises, is open too and giving vent to his own howl, beyond his control, forcing its way up and out of the depths.

He is overcome by a sensation of falling, as if his body is spinning into a vast bottomless space. He spirals further and further down into the huge emptiness, the appalling sights and sounds becoming fainter until they are finally lost in a dark silence.

★

There is a long pause. With an effort Thomas looks up. He sees Macpherson sitting back in his chair with his hands behind his head, eyes closed and face tilted up towards the ceiling. Eventually his eyes open and he faces Thomas. The younger man looks down at the floor between them, avoiding the gaze.

For a minute or two the doctor sits still, his hands flat on the desk in front of him, his eyes shifting their focus to some point above and beyond the door of the room. Thomas looks up at him in the silence, trying without success to read the older man's expression.

Finally the difficult silence ends.

'That must have been a harrowing experience for you to go through and I imagine that reviving the memory of it now must be deeply disturbing, too. You are likely to have those images recurring quite often now that they have come to the surface. You will need to make use of the same strategies I gave you earlier, to soften their impact a little. It's not good to be overwhelmed by them. I think, from what I've gathered before, that you've been managing this problem quite well. You'll need to keep doing the same.

'Tell me, now that you have it clear and fresh in your mind, what do you feel about it at this moment?'

Thomas considers. What does he feel? There's a peculiar sensation of emptiness. As if he is feeling nothing, in a space where he might be expected to feel something. He looks down, wondering how much of this he should reveal.

'I don't know. I feel empty.'

'Very well. You feel empty. That is one feeling. And it is not surprising, when these memories have been released from a space where you have shut them away for months. Now what else do you feel? Or think? What comes to your mind to say about it all? About what you did.' He pauses, considers, and adds, 'and what you didn't do.'

Thomas hesitates, turning those last added words over in his mind. Suddenly his mind is flooded by the image of the rocky shore, the outer reef, the channel between, the swells breaking on the reef and foaming over into the channel. He sees Jane clinging to the reef, face turned towards him, one arm waving, hears her screaming to him for help. Feels his back pressed against the wall of rock.

He looks up into the older man's face, searching for a way to express the overwhelming confusion of thoughts and feelings crowding his mind, finding nothing to offer but trivial words suitable for some minor misdemeanour.

'I feel guilty. I ought to have done something to help her.' He hears the weakness, the inadequacy in his words.

Macpherson sits back in his chair, letting a long breath out. 'Ah, yes. You feel guilty. I would like you to explore that feeling a little, if you don't mind. I can see two different aspects of the situation, and I want us to look at them separately.

'To begin with we'll leave you out of it, and think simply about what is happening to Jane. Try to imagine yourself in her position. You are Jane, in the water being dragged through the gap in the reef. A huge wave breaks over your head, and you're forced under. Don't talk about it; just try to feel what she would be feeling in those moments.'

Eyes closed, Thomas imagines the immense power of the breaking wave churning around and above him, the loss of any sense of where the surface is through the opaque foam, the desperation to struggle towards air, to breathe, the panic.

He opens his eyes, looking towards the doctor again

'She must have been—it must have been terrifying for her.'

'Very well. She would certainly have been terrified. But were you responsible for her being in that terrifying situation?'

Thomas looks at the older man, unsure where the exchange is heading. 'No, I suppose not. Certainly not.'

Macpherson leans forward, fixing Thomas with a steady gaze. 'Precisely so. But surely feelings of guilt are only appropriate when you are responsible for something; when you've done something that other people would have reason to blame you for.

You were not to blame for her being caught in the rip and dragged into the surf, were you? Surely you can't reasonably feel guilty about an unpredictable accident such as that.'

The younger man looks down at the floor for a few moments, then meets the doctor's eyes. 'I suppose that's right. Yes.'

'So, let's push this a little further. Imagine Jane again, as she is dragged under the water, struggling to breathe, finally unable to get back to the surface, and drowning. You have set your feeling of guilt aside, because there is no place for it. What are you feeling now about what is happening to her?'

Thomas closes his eyes and sits back in the chair imagining her desperation, her last breath, the uncontrollable gasp that fills her lungs with water, finally the merciful fading of consciousness.

He opens his eyes again and looks across at Macpherson.

'It's a horrible way to die, drowning. Full of terror. Beyond that, it's just so sad to think that she's gone.' His voice trembles.

The doctor sits back in his chair, taking in a deep breath and letting it out slowly.

'It must be very upsetting to recover these memories. It looks to me as if your feeling of guilt has been focused mainly on the fact that you held back from swimming out and trying to help her. Is that so?'

Thomas looks away to the side, avoiding a response.

Macpherson continues, 'I have the impression that your religion has provided you with a rather judgmental God who makes laws and punishes people who break them. I would like you to imagine for a moment a rather different sort of God who wants all his creatures to enjoy as much well-being as possible. Is such a God likely to blame you for holding back? As you described the incident, the young woman was in an extremely dangerous situation, verging on hopeless. She was apparently a competent swimmer, but she couldn't save herself. If you had swum out to help, the most likely outcome would have been that two young people drowned, rather than one. And the world would have been worse off for that. I read about a case very much like that only a couple of weeks ago down near Margaret River. Why would a benevolent God blame you for not doubling the tragedy? When you think about it, don't you see that what you did was probably the best option in a desperate situation. That doesn't leave much room for feeling ashamed, or guilty, does it?'

Thomas shakes his head, feeling just a little calmer.

'You came to me in the beginning with a quite specific problem, to do with repressed memories. Now your lost memories are recovered—the crucial parts at least. I didn't expect it to be a very difficult task. It's only been, what? Three and a half months? Four?'

Thomas nods without meeting the other man's eyes. 'About that.'

'I take it that you will be going to your archbishop with this story now that it's been recovered. I'm not sure who else you will speak to. Of course you will need to make a statement to the police, to bring some sort of finality to their investigation. Feel free to refer them to me if they want a supporting statement about the recovery of your lost memories. The unexplained disappearance of anyone is primarily police business, not the archbishop's business. They will need a formal statement, but I am more interested in what your religious advisers have to say about the events and what you think about their advice, after a little time for reflection.'

Thomas listens. *Religious advisers.* He thought he caught an odd tone in the way Macpherson used the expression.

'At our first meeting,' the doctor continues, 'I told you that I saw the possibility of uncovering wider issues in your life than this matter of recovering your missing memories. You might think that this is really beyond my brief, so to speak, but I'd see it as part of my professional obligation to pursue one set of ideas a short distance with you. I suggest that we should have at least one more meeting. I will see you at the same time next week, and we will talk about the response from your church to the memories that have been retrieved, as well as opening up some more general questions. It would be a good thing if we could continue to meet beyond next week to explore these larger issues in your life, but that may not be possible, given that we have finished the task set by your archbishop.'

★

Thomas walks out onto the street and turns towards the bus stop. A feeling of relief is creeping over him as he contemplates, beyond the coming unavoidable interviews with the archbishop and the police, the end of this terrible saga. The police interview will be difficult, but the story he has to tell is not as black as some people might have suspected. There have probably been dreadful rumours circulating in some quarters about what he is supposed to have done.

The sense that relief and finality are at last coming into view is suddenly swept away as Thomas's mind is filled again by the image of a huge wave poised to break, and in the face of the wave, a head: Jane's head. And her arm waving, and her voice, shrill with terror. Her last words, crying out to him for help.

13

Confession

Father Kevin sits back and runs one hand across the top of his narrow bald head and sighs.

'My God, m'boy, there's another two or three dozen hairs gone every day. I'd be able to count what's left one by one except that they're all around the back.' He grins. 'But getting back to the main point—that's it, is it? What you've told me? Is that the extent of what happened?'

Thomas clasps his hands together tightly between his knees.

'I think so. Or really, I'm sure. Yes. All that's important, anyway.' He looks up from the floor but can't quite bring himself to meet those small eyes.

'And you had really forgotten all this? That's remarkable. Maybe the witch-doctor knows a trick or two after all. I'd taken him to be nothing but a fashionable fake. Judge not, that ye be not judged. It goes to show that we can learn something new every day. Maybe a small celebration is called for. Your lost days have been found again. They've returned, like the prodigal son. Or was it the prodigal sheep? Let's have just a spot of that Vat 69.'

Father Kevin heads for the bottle standing on the kitchen bench and pours two rather unequal spots.

'There you are, m'boy. I don't think you really enjoyed your first experience with it a week or two ago. But you should try again. Persevere in the path of virtue. A parish priest needs to learn how to drink; there aren't many pleasures available in this job.' He grins, holding out the Vegemite glass with the smaller share. To Thomas, who finally manages for a moment to look him in the eye, it doesn't seem an altogether happy grin.

The small man takes a careful sip.

'Now, talking about parish priests, I can't see any problem about your being one, and I'm sure the archbishop will take the same view when he hears your story. I take it that you will be speaking to him soon. And so will I.'

Thomas mutters something: an indeterminate sound that might suggest that he's grateful, or just that he's heard.

'And on the subject of clean bills of health, you'd be looking to me to say something as your spiritual director, and confessor.'

Thomas looks down at the floor again.

'I'm sure you don't need me to lay it out for you in detail. You've done the course in moral theology more recently than me, and the rules can't have changed to any extent. Still, maybe you need to hear it said.'

Father Kevin looks past Thomas to the window and the world beyond it. To the younger man, who takes a quick side-long glance at him, he doesn't look as if his whole mind is focused on this task.

'So, you didn't try to pull that young lady out of the water. There's no sin in that. I'm not a swimmer m'self, but I take it that there'd be some considerable risk in it. For you, I mean. Nobody's obliged to risk his own life to try to save someone else's. No doubt a hero would have done it. But it's no sin not to be a hero. The Church's teaching is quite clear about this, as you know very well. There are obligations, and there are counsels of perfection. This was not an obligation.

'In fact, when you think about it, maybe the whole thing was providential, the way it worked out. Maybe it was God holding you back from playing the hero. All that contact with a young lady: it could easily have gone to the head of a young fellow who's not used to it. You might have been tempted away from your religious vocation if it had gone on much longer. I thought I picked up a few hints along those lines, you know, while you were telling the story.'

The priest's small eyes focus obliquely on Thomas, with a momentary sly grin, which is replaced by a more earnest expression.

'But look at what happened. The source of the temptation is gone, and you're still here, setting out on a life devoted to God's work. Saved by your own hesitation, in fact. The finger of God, perhaps, holding you back, so that you will go on to do his work. A blessing, really.

'The self-abuse, now: that's a different matter. Holy purity. There's no such thing as a venial sin against the virtue of holy purity. All sins of impurity are grave, as you well know. And when I think about it there's another blessing in what happened: the finger of God holding you back from the danger of dying with a grave sin on your soul.'

Father Kevin is looking through the window towards the street again although he seems to be focusing on something outside that Thomas can't see. His voice has taken on an almost automatic tone, as if his thoughts are a long way away.

'A grave sin, yes. But God knows that we are all weak, all sinners. You're sorry, no doubt? Repentant? Determined not to fall again? And to avoid the occasions of sin? Well, you will have no difficulty avoiding that particular occasion of sin. Very well, then. For a penance, say two decades of the Rosary.'

The little man swings into the absolution: *'Ego te absolvo,* I wash you clean from your sins in the name of the Father and of the Son and of the Holy Ghost.' The Latin formula flows easily off his tongue.

Thomas, too, looks out of the window as the ritual words flow past him. There is a degree of relief in the beginning of the end of this horrific saga. But he still has a feeling of incompleteness: a sense that something is not settled by this rehearsal of the familiar rules and ritual words.

'Yes, I know all that. But I can't get the pictures out of my mind, or the sounds. Not since the memories came back. Her head in the foam at the gap in the reef, with one arm waving. Then she appears again out of a huge wave that's about to break over her, looking towards me, and calling to me. Screaming for help. I feel desperate to do something, but somehow I can't. I remember setting out to swim to her, but next moment pulling back. Backwards and forwards like that five or six times. More. And then she is gone. But I'm still here. Perhaps I couldn't have helped her, really, but I feel something shrinking inside when I think of myself not even trying.'

The older man makes an impatient sound.

'Yes, yes. It's very distressing, I'm sure. But that has nothing to do with what we are concerned with here. The rules. What the rules say about that situation is quite clear.'

He drains the last drops in his glass.

'Here, have another spot of this Vat 69. But I see that you've hardly touched your first. I think I will all the same.' He pours himself another careful half-inch and looks gloomily at the level in the bottle. 'Nearly half-empty already. I'll have to take this slowly; God alone knows where the next bottle is coming from.'

Thomas takes a sip from his own glass. He's still not sure about it. Perhaps in time he'll make up his mind about whisky. And about a few other matters that used to seem clear, but are recently becoming hazy.

14

Final Consultation

Macpherson is sitting back in his chair with his eyes directed at the ceiling above Thomas's head, but their focus appears to be far out beyond the confines of the room. He waits for the younger man to add to what he has said, waits a full minute and more, but no more comes. He sits forward, forearms on the desk, looking at Thomas in silence.

Eventually he shakes his head.

'That is extraordinary, if I have understood it properly. Is this the judgment of your religious adviser, that masturbation is a grave sin, but the drowning of the young lady was a blessing? Did he really say that it was providential that you couldn't bring yourself to try to help her? Because you will go on to pursue a career in your Church? Is that the way he spoke? A providential blessing! I'm sure you know that most people would see what happened as a real tragedy. Would you expect other people of your persuasion to think along the same lines as this man?'

Thomas nods, looking away.

'The archbishop—I had a meeting with him yesterday. He seemed . . . I suppose he seemed relieved by what I told him.

He said that this outcome was . . . I think his word was *satisfactory*. From his point of view. He said that he looked forward to ordaining me now that any obstacles are out of the way. He may have thought of Jane as a potential obstacle. Quite possibly.'

The older man stands.

'Did neither of these gentlemen express any sense of how tragic the drowning of this young woman was? That is truly extraordinary. I would never have imagined that anyone could be so unfeeling. And what did you feel, when you heard them speak like that?'

Thomas looks up to find the doctor's eyes are looking at him intensely. He hesitates before replying.

'I couldn't get those pictures out of my mind—you know, the waves breaking on the reef, Jane, clinging to the rock and then being swept out over jagged outcrops. I was imagining what it would feel like for me, being dragged over those rocks. I could hear her calling to me just an instant before the last wave broke. I was seeing and hearing all that while they were talking to me, both of them and I felt as if—this is hard to explain—as if what they were saying came from somewhere a long way away. It didn't seem to connect with what I was seeing, and telling them about. It wasn't quite like that when I went to the police. They kept me there a couple of hours going over and over what happened, and all the time I could see it as if I was still there watching it happen. But the police—this is hard to explain, too—they seemed to be closer to seeing what I was seeing. Focused on what actually happened to Jane, and the sadness of it, not on how the church might be affected.'

Macpherson turns and walks the two or three steps to the window and stands with his back to Thomas, looking out to the trees and unkempt grass in the overgrown garden. Thomas watches him, puzzled. Wondering what he could be thinking. Why he is silent for so long.

The doctor turns back but remains standing, outlined by the window. With the light behind him, his expression is hard to read. He moves to his chair and eventually sits, seeming just a little more relaxed.

'You have spoken about sins several times. I think I told you at the beginning that I had no use for the word in my professional vocabulary. I said so, and I thought so, at the time. As far as possible I try to understand without judging—without blame. And to help anyone who consults me to understand in the same spirit. But now I find . . . I am not quite sure what I find. I think I find myself strongly driven to judge.

'This is not directed at you personally, you must understand. It is for, perhaps I should say, a whole culture. I think you are beginning to find your way out of it, but you have come to me from a culture that seems to turn a good half of what I understand to be morality, completely upside down. Pain is good, pleasure is bad. Masturbation, for instance. Why on earth should anyone be taught to feel guilty about it, when I suppose everyone does it, and it harms nobody? The problem seems to be that it's a source of pleasure. Other things struck me too. In this scheme of things it seems that ritual is more important than helping anyone. People who live celibate lives turned in on themselves are reckoned to be better than people who share their lives with someone else and help to raise children. On a trivial level, a man who destroys an apple, rather than eating it or giving it to someone else, should be admired. And the one who was so intent on following his own plans that he passed by a last opportunity to visit his old mother? I would say that he was self-absorbed almost to a pathological degree, but apparently he's a saint.

'Your culture seems to worship a God that I find very disturbing. I gather that this God is pleased when his devotees have dreadful deaths inflicted on them for no obvious advantage to anyone. And when they torture themselves and mutilate their own bodies. Your book was obviously written by a person with a very strange fascination with pain, and he clearly imagines a God who shares the same fascination. It seems that the same characteristic—I'd class it as a pathology—runs strongly through your tradition.

'Take for example, the saint in last week's story: Saint Peter somebody. I heard a mention of his hair shirt, that he inherited from some other saint whose name escapes me now. I'm sure I've heard about hair shirts before, but I've never understood exactly what they were, or are.'

Thomas feels the familiar prickle of embarrassment at the back of his neck.

'A hair shirt is something that some people—holy men, I suppose I'd call them—used to wear next to the skin. They were made out of coarse, prickly hair—goat hair I think it was. So that they would feel scratchy and uncomfortable.'

'I see. Now what would be the point of it?'

Macpherson's mouth is twisted just a little, in an expression suggesting amusement? Distaste? Thomas can't decide.

'It was an act of penance. Self-denial. Mortification of the flesh.' He listens to the stock phrases emerging from his mouth, wondering how they will be understood, and adds, 'Some of them—the saints, I mean—vowed when they put their hair shirts on that they would never take them off.' He worries instantly about why he added that piece of information. What will Macpherson make of it?

The older man's expression surely has a touch of distaste about it now.

'I see. That's interesting. Another form of self-inflicted torture I'd have to call it, I suppose. As an aspect of saintliness. If they stayed on permanently they must have ended up in a thoroughly unsavoury condition, the saints and the hair shirts both. The hair shirts probably came to be more alive than the saints.' The shape of his mouth suggests a swing from distaste to amusement. 'As for inheriting one that had been on somebody else for twenty or thirty years—no wonder the poor fellow didn't survive for long after that.'

'There was something else about last week's saint that caught my attention. It was to do with the relics. As far as I could make out these were parts of his body. Have I understood this properly, that they sometimes dismembered the corpses of holy men and parcelled out the body parts to places here and there that had a claim to a piece?'

Thomas is aware of something much sharper than mere curiosity behind the question. He answers cautiously.

'This used to be done centuries ago. As far as I know, nobody does it now.'

'I would imagine not. But apparently people still venerate the ancient body parts. Still hope for miracles from them as if there's some magical power embedded in them. To me, you know, this all seems quite macabre.'

Thomas shifts uncomfortably in his chair. He hesitates, unsure how to respond.

'Relics like those—and the miracles people pray for, Catholics aren't obliged to believe everything like that.'

'I would hope not.' Macpherson smiles. 'Anyway, how can anyone oblige you to believe anything? Don't you believe on account of the reasons? The evidence? Rather than because someone tells you to believe.'

Thomas is floundering, drowning in all these questions, these challenges. They come from another world. His neck feels sweaty inside the rigid clerical collar. He realises that his hands are clenched into tight fists and tries to relax them. He can find no response. For half a minute or so neither man speaks.

Macpherson brings an end to the silence.

'I've been doing a little reading of my own about the saints. Just for background. I've worked through twenty-five or thirty of them but I haven't found one yet who lived anything like what I'd call a normal human life. How do they get to be considered saints?'

Thomas shifts uncomfortably in his chair, hesitates before answering.

'Their lives have been examined. People are canonised on account of the holiness of their lives, basically.'

'That doesn't help me a lot. I don't have a sense of what you mean by holiness. If you told me that a holy person has to keep away from lying, cheating, malice, selfishness, cruelty, and so on, I would have some grasp of what you mean. And the point of holding them up as models. But the saints I've heard and read about, their qualifications for the position are completely different. They seem to have got the job mainly by giving up the most innocent pleasure, and even basic comfort, turning their backs on sexual activity even in the most proper context, having nothing to do with reproduction and family life, and even close personal relationships generally. If that is what makes for holiness, then I don't see the point of it, or the point of admiring it.

'Well, never mind. I was wondering, you see, whether there were any saints who lived ordinary lives, as sons or daughters, husbands or wives, fathers or mothers, and so on, but did it all particularly well. I mean being especially kind, unselfish, honest, responsible. Qualities that everyone admires. Do you see what I mean? Saints who were simply thoroughly decent, normal human beings living normal human lives, instead of all this pain-worship, this masochism.' He shuts his mouth decisively, as if he has to bite off the rest of what he was going to say. Then continues, 'But I see that I was mistaken to let my curiosity carry me away.

'We've heard a lot about pain in your book, and I've had rather a lot to say about it myself. We can't get through a life without pain, of course. We need it to tell us to take a hand off the hot stove, or to rest a sprained ankle. And there's another sort of pain that we feel when we lose someone we love. We wouldn't choose not to feel it, even if we had the option, because if we felt nothing, that would strip the meaning from our lives. But we don't cultivate that sort of pain for its own sake. It's just an inevitable part of the normal pattern of human life. It's bound up with love. There's enough pain in the ordinary way of things that can't be avoided, without inflicting it on ourselves deliberately.'

He pauses. Thomas looks up for a moment. The older man's face is turned aside, as if he is trying to hide the intensity of a feeling that he is struggling to control. Thomas looks at his averted face, wondering about the source of this feeling, beyond anything in his own experience.

Macpherson seems to recover his composure and goes on.

'The worship of a God who is supposed to look favourably on all of this—pain, and blood, and withdrawal from normal human relationships and feelings and obligations—if I had any use for the word *blasphemy*, I'd say this was blasphemous. But I suppose I'd have to be a believer to talk about blasphemy. Leaving any God out of it, to me a great deal of this is incomprehensible. There's an inhuman streak in it. And sometimes, I have to say, perverted.' The Scottish rolled *r* comes through very strongly in that last word, giving it even more emphasis.

Thomas listens in silence, sitting rigidly upright on the edge of that awkward chair. He is astonished at the power of feeling in the outburst he has heard. And yet why is it that he can say nothing in response? He struggles without success to think of any saint who was canonised for the qualities Macpherson admires—as he pointed out, qualities that everyone admires. He sits silent, trying to close a door on the questions, shut them into a space at the back of his mind.

Macpherson runs the fingers of both hands through his hair and sits back in his chair.

'I probably ought to apologise. As I've understood my profession up until now, a psychoanalyst is not expected to behave like this. We're supposed to maintain a detached, objective attitude as far as possible. I've never reacted like this before—not in twenty-five years. I shall have to think about why I've lost my detachment. There may be something else going on that I haven't thought out properly. It's possible that I'm coming to think that it's not realistic to avoid judgment regardless of what comes to light. Maybe even my calling has room for a little blaming on occasion, when the situation cries out for it. Perhaps I can find a use for the idea of sin after all. Or *wickedness* might be a better word; it's less ecclesiastical.

'This doesn't sit well with what I was taught—what I've believed myself until now. But we all have to take a hard look occasionally at what we've been taught, what we've believed until now. Including myself.'

The older man flexes his shoulders, stretches his arms up and to the side, bends his neck left and right, and smiles at Thomas.

'I obviously need to loosen up a little. That's more than enough about me. And probably about your Church, too. We need to get the focus back onto you. The drowning of that young lady down on the south coast—it must have been a terrible experience for you to witness that. And to be unable to do anything about it. The plane crash too. The horror of it all would be enough to account for your memories being shut away, but something else might have been at work as well. I wonder whether those experiences sparked some ideas in you that you were not quite ready to deal with consciously, because they had the potential to disrupt the existing shape of your life. Repressed memories and ideas are still there, in some way, and they tend to come out in disguise, in dreams.

'As you were telling the story last week, what struck me most was your inability to act decisively. It would have been a difficult situation for anyone—to try to help or not. I don't know what I would have done. I'm not suggesting that you made the wrong choice, as I said earlier. But as you described the situation you couldn't choose at all: couldn't make a decision one way or the other. So the events just swept on past you. Is this the way you would see it?'

Thomas considers, nods agreement, recalling vividly the sensation of paralysis, physical and mental, the fruitless churning of his thoughts, as the tragedy unfolded in front of him.

Macpherson nods too.

'Yes. While I was absorbing that part of the story I thought about the dreams you have described to me over the last few weeks. I'd like to put some ideas to you about them—ideas about a more general problem you might have in dealing with decisions. These are not for you to respond to now—just to take away and consider whether they make any sense to you.

You told me about two dreams that were very similar in some ways. You were floating in water in both of them, and the water was carrying you along with it, though you had no sensation of moving until you looked around at the surroundings. In the first you were floating along a narrow channel between high banks. In the second it was a wide open expanse of ocean that you were drifting across. The central thing that struck me in both of them was that you were not in control of the situation. You weren't so much moving, as being moved by a force outside you. What do you think lies behind these dreams? To me they suggest that you have a concern, below the level of your conscious thinking, that your life is not under your control—that you are not making decisions about your pathway through life—just drifting, following a course set for you by other people. That is, in the first of them. In the second your direction was not hemmed in by high banks,

175

but you still had no control over it, and no idea where the drift was taking you.

'Then there's your dream about the high hedge along the seminary boundary, and your finding an old gateway entangled in it: a gateway that you hadn't noticed before. And it's so overgrown with shrubbery that it's almost impassable. It seems to me that this dream has strong links with the other two. What does it suggest to you? Could the overgrown gateway symbolise the possibility of other paths through life that might open up on the other side? An unconscious wish to explore other ways, other sorts of experience that have been shut off to you?

Putting these dreams together, do you think they might give a hint that, deep down, your view of your future is not as clear as it used to be? And that, on the same deep level, you have a subconscious sense that there might be some decisions you need to make about the shape of your life?'

Macpherson sits back in his chair. He looks to Thomas to be more relaxed.

'I have presented you with some questions about your whole life that I know could possibly be as confronting for you in their own way as the memories that you have recovered over these months. And I've asked you to take these questions away and think about them. You may find this a seriously disturbing task, on top of coping with the memories that are bound to keep recurring. You are welcome to come back to me if you feel the need to talk over the issues that I think are facing you. And while I began this afternoon with some rather intemperate talk, I hope that you won't entirely forget what I said then.'

He looks directly into Thomas's eyes.

'Finally, if we don't meet each other again, I wish you good luck in your calling. Whatever it might turn out to be, in the end.'

Walking out to the street, Thomas turns over in his mind Macpherson's final words. *His calling, whatever it might turn out to be, in the end.* He wonders whether this man can see something looming in his future that he himself is at present unable to imagine.

15

Revelation

Thomas steps off the bus and checks his watch. Thanks to the shorter consultation he'll be back a good hour earlier than in the previous weeks. He steps out briskly on the twenty-minute walk. It's a cooler afternoon; autumn is setting in at last.

He thinks about that outburst of Macpherson's about the church—intemperate, he had called it himself. The thought brings out a flock of questions that he had tried to cage at the back of his mind. They circle around inside his head. What *is* the reason for admiring a man who wastes an apple rather than eating it or giving it to someone else? Or another who refuses to visit his mother because he is so busy at the Lord's work. Is it possible that the Lord would have been better pleased with him visiting his mother? What would Thomas's own mother have thought about it? And why would we believe in a God who is gratified to see people suffer—at the hands of other people or at their own hands. Hair shirts, and fasting nearly to the point of starvation. And worse. Whips: self-flagellation, not unknown among the saints. Not uncommon, in fact. Not all of it in the ancient times, either.

And what would Macpherson say if he heard the story of the local priest who was found when he died, so it is said, to have a small wooden cross nailed to his back? In place for a long time. Old ulcers, probably stinking. Perhaps that is what killed him. The cross is rumoured to be stored somewhere in the diocesan archives waiting to be produced as a valuable holy relic when the man is declared a saint. The story has been passed around locally for years among the most devout, with a sense of wonder at the thought of treading the same ground that has been trodden by a holy man whose life was lived in the tradition of the saints of ancient times.

What was Macpherson's word? *Perverted*. From a Latin root. Turned the wrong way. Twisted. Is it possible that all of this is twisted in the wrong direction? He shakes his head to dislodge the unsettling thoughts, turning his attention to the real world. There is the house of the young mother with the bikini. Thomas's pace slows. But there's nobody in sight this afternoon. Perhaps the little fellow has a rest after lunch. What would his mother be doing now? Possibly resting too? On her bed? Their bed, hers and her husband's?

He remembers Macpherson wishing him good luck in his calling—whatever it might turn out to be in the end. He wonders. How do two people decide that their calling is to marry? How would the course of his life so far have had to be different, for him to be looking towards marriage instead of ordination? The world of shared homes and shared beds and shared lives, it's unexplored territory for him. He wonders how people find their way into it.

He quickens his stride, trying to leave the fantasy image behind him, hearing the clomping sound of his thick-soled black shoes on the paving slabs and feeling the bottoms of his trouser-legs flap awkwardly as he steps out with a determined briskness.

Turning in at the church gate, as usual, he half-shuts his eyes and lets his gaze drift out of focus, looking for the real church shining through this ugly grey shed of a building. And there it is, the remembered fantasy: the carved stone, the spires, the gargoyles, the saints' statues, the windows with light in them and more saints glowing in stained glass. But it all seems hazier than before, less sharply defined, as if drifting further away on an invisible current. The austere liturgical chant of his imagination is almost inaudible.

He heads past the church towards the presbytery, passing the front room window on his way to the door. His footsteps are almost silent on the bare ground and dried grass that could in other hands be a front garden. It's not only Father Kevin; Thomas can think of a few other Catholic churches set in barren surroundings like these. And those set in well-maintained gardens are generally in parishes wealthy enough to employ a gardener. How many priests are gardeners themselves? He can think of one, among dozens who are not.

His eye is caught by some activity inside the front room. Curtains screen most of the window except for a small gap in the centre. There seem to be rhythmical movements going on inside, but he can't see what is moving, or who. It is difficult to make out any forms in the dim interior, but perhaps there is a head.

He moves closer to the window, stepping carefully to avoid noise and keeping to one side, letting the curtains screen his approach. He leans momentarily to the centre for a quick glimpse.

There are two heads in view. One of them, facing away from him, is the unmistakeable narrow bald pate of Father Kevin, with its sparse rear fringe of hair showing above the back of a chair. The other is a smaller head, facing to the side of the room.

Thomas chances a step to the centre of the window for a longer look. His eyes are beginning to adjust to the dimmer light inside. The smaller head is a boy's, familiar, though only part of the face is in sight. Of course. The Regan boy, Michael, the youngest altar boy.

He is sitting sideways on the small man's lap. The priest's right hand seems to be holding the hand of the boy, moving it. The hands themselves are out of sight, but from behind Thomas can see the two arms moving rhythmically, up, down, up, down. As the arms move, Father Kevin's head and shoulders rock in time; back and forth, back and forth. A physical sense of disgust rises in Thomas's throat. The sound of regular heavy panting comes faintly through the window. On the boy's cheek there are the faint tracks of tears. Noticing them, Thomas feels a surge of anger; his stomach muscles tense, his fists clench wanting to strike out.

The rhythm of the movements becomes faster. The small man's whole body writhes, jerks convulsively, then relaxes with a long out-breath that can be heard clearly outside. Then for half a minute or so the two inside are motionless, and Thomas is caught between disbelief and horror. Is this a figment of his imagination? He reaches out to touch the window-frame to be sure that what he has been watching is part of the real world.

The frozen moment is splintered suddenly. The boy half-turns his head, sees Thomas staring through the window, slips abruptly off Father Kevin's lap. The priest struggles to his feet and turns to the window, eyes wide with alarm. His hands are scrabbling to cram a limp pinkish member back into his trousers.

While the room dissolves into movement, the boy scurrying toward the door into the passage, the small man fumbling with the disarray of his trousers, Thomas remains at the window, watching the appalling scene as if from a distance, on a screen. He feels still frozen into position, all his muscles tense, his mind, too, as if paralysed.

Then, quite suddenly, he begins to see the situation as if from a different location. He can't remain simply a passive viewer, looking in from the outside. He is part of that scene, involved in it. It demands action from him. He takes a step away from the window and towards the front door, then hesitates, unable to visualise what he will do once inside. He turns and begins walking out towards the street and away, wanting more time to think. But before he reaches the footpath he realises that he must confront this situation now. He must take a first decisive step, and what will follow in the wake of that step will, he supposes, show itself. He turns back up the presbytery path. Opens the door and sees the Regan boy slinking out the back.

He steps into the front room. Father Kevin finishes scrabbling with his trouser buttons and looks up. Thomas stands silent, just inside the room, looking at the scrawny little man. He watches the priest turning his face away, looking down, trying with one hand to hide the small wet patch on his trousers, and succeeding only in drawing Thomas's attention to it.

After a long awkward silence the priest speaks.

'You're back early, aren't you? I wasn't expecting you till later. I was just talking to him, you know. About being a priest—going to the seminary.'

Thomas looks at the scrawny shoulders, the narrow face, the pot belly, the bald pate. He shakes his head. The older man looks away, silent for a moment, then tries again. There's an unpleasant sharpness in his voice.

'He wanted to, you know. He started it. All over me. I could hardly stop him.'

Thomas watches the petty man protesting, looking away, avoiding his eyes. What is this feeling: *contempt? disgust?* Anger takes over; the bitter taste of bile rises from his throat onto his tongue. He shakes his head again in silence. There are no words that he can find to say to this despicable wretch.

Father Kevin takes a few steps to the window and stares out at the street for a couple of silent minutes. When he turns back his face wears a ghost of the familiar one-sided grin. Even at its best it is not, as the younger man has noticed before, an entirely happy grin and it is far from its best at this moment.

'Well, m'boy. No point in protesting, I suppose. Caught red handed, so to speak.' He glances at his hand, the hand that was forcing the hand of the Regan boy. Wipes it against his trouser leg. 'I'm off to the kitchen. There's a bit of that Vat 69 left, I think. There'll never be a better time to finish it off. You'll join me?'

The joviality doesn't sound convincing. Thomas wonders whether it is ever real. He holds back in the doorway, watching as the narrow bald head and the puny shoulders retreat down the passage to the kitchen. How can he understand this miserable figure as the same man who stands tall in the pulpit in splendid robes every Sunday morning haranguing his congregation about their moral duties—and sits in the confessional listening to their outpourings of guilt? And judging them. It is all unintelligible. Thomas is unable to see what he is going to do about the situation, but certain that he must do something.

First, though, he must try to get his head clearer—find some less confused understanding of what he has stumbled on. He follows down the passage, treading tentatively, uncertain what he will say or do when he gets to the end of it, arriving in the kitchen to hear the small priest set the bottle and two Vegemite glasses down on the table with a thump.

'There we are. Half a bottle left, a bit more in fact. That's better than I thought. Thank God.'

He pours a cautious splash into one glass and a more generous ration into the other, keeping his eyes fixed on the task. He pushes the smaller share towards the younger man and slumps down in a chair with his own. Thomas watches the glass being slid towards him and pushes it away. How can he accept anything from that hand?

Taking a careful sip, Father Kevin stares out through the kitchen window at the fence that separates the church property from the neighbours. He finishes his drink with one gulp and pours himself another.

Finally the priest turns back to look Thomas in the face. The younger man turns his head away, feeling as he does so an onset of dizziness. Everything that has surrounded and shaped his life seems to be crumbling. The words of the familiar hymn come back to him: *Change and decay in all around I see. Oh Thou who changest not . . .* The flow of words dries up. Thomas is taken over by a strange sensation, as if he is falling into empty space. He grasps the edge of the table; at least that feels solid and dependable. Pulls out a chair and sits to save himself from falling.

The small man speaks. The trace of strained joviality has gone altogether. He sounds tired, sad.

'I don't know what you're thinking. About all of this.'

He swallows another mouthful of whisky, looks despondently at the bottle, finishes what is left of his second drink and pours himself a full glass, gulping down a substantial part of it.

'It's not much fun, you know, being a parish priest. Especially in a place like this. I mean, look at it.' He gestures around the room.

Thomas looks around, following the gesture. It is certainly a mean little room. Fibro walls peeling, sadly in need of new paint. A fly-spotted framed print of a photograph of the pope hanging on one wall: Pius the Twelfth, looking, as always, lean, cold and remote. The lino on the floor is stained and cracked, almost worn through in the doorway and in front of the sink. The window looking out to the side fence is grimy and the dust coats the sill thickly, causing it to look stone grey.

The young man shakes his head.

'Yes, but what I saw. How could anyone do that? How could you?'

Father Kevin sighs. Pours the last of the whisky into his glass and drains it in one mouthful, turning aside to stare out of the kitchen window for a full minute before responding.

'What am I going to say? How could I do it? I don't know. I tell myself I'll never do it again. Every time. Well, nearly every time. But somehow I do.' He turns towards Thomas with a faint hint of the same old grin. 'Just can't help myself, I suppose.'

185

Thomas, listening, is beginning to grasp the dimensions of what he's stumbled on. The incident seen through the front room window comes back to him, and with it the sensation of repugnance.

'You mean you've done this before?'

'You didn't know? I wondered whether you'd have heard the story from someone. Some of it anyway. The old archbishop tried to keep it all quiet. Moved me on three or four times. Plenty of people seem to know something. You'd have heard sooner or later.

'Why do you think I'm in this godforsaken parish, with hardly two pennies to rub together? And me nearly sixty. I should have been in a decent parish fifteen years ago. Like Bayview—nice house, housekeeper, gardener, a couple of curates and plenty of money coming in. I drove past that place last week when I took a Holden for a test drive. I tell you, m'boy, it brought tears to my eyes just to look at it. A big wide double garage with one of them big Fords in it—the new model. Shiny black. And a new Holden for second-best. Both of them paid for in cash, I suppose. And me getting knocked back for a loan on a Holden, even a demo car.'

The little man picks up his glass again but finds it empty; then he reaches over the table for Thomas's glass, draining it in one gulp. Puts the bottle to his lips to salvage the last few drops. 'All gone. Sad.' He stands and takes a couple of steps to the corner of the room to drop the empty bottle into the bin. It hits the rim as it falls, and tumbles inside with a clatter. 'Clumsy me.'

He returns to the table, stumbling against his chair on the way. Just over half a bottle of whisky in fifteen minutes is much more than he is used to. And on an empty stomach.

'There's one blessing: the boy won't tell his parents. A strange little boy, he is. Hardly a word to say for himself—God knows why. And if he did tell them they probably wouldn't believe him. Good Irish Catholics. Won't say a word against the priest.

'Still, you can never be sure what people are going to do. Like the last time I got shifted. Good Catholic parents they were, too. You'd have thought so anyway. But off they scuttled, straight to the archbishop, the old one. And here I am in this rat-hole.'

He looks around the room, running one hand across his bald head. He turns suddenly towards Thomas, his small eyes narrow, suspicious, almost hostile.

'You wouldn't be thinking of it yourself, by any chance—turning me in—would you?' The sharp unpleasant tone is back in the small man's voice.

Thomas spreads his hands out, looking towards the window. He can think of nothing to say. He knows he will do something, but what?

'You might, eh? I'll deny it, you know. Swear by all the powers. I'll swear I found you at it yourself. Only trying to shift the blame onto me. That's what I'll tell them. You'll regret it.' His small mouth is half-open, teeth showing, eyes cunning.

Just as suddenly the blustering and bravado disappear. He wilts. Rests his elbows on the table, his chin on his hands.

'No. That wouldn't wash. They'd never believe it, would they? Not after all the other stuff. I'd be out, you know. This new archbishop—I don't know that he's been told anything. I think they tried to keep him in the dark about it, with him coming from elsewhere. Clean slate and all that. But it would all come out soon enough.' There are tears in his eyes.

'He wouldn't shift me again, he'd just kick me out. And where would I go? This place might be a rat-hole but at least it's a place. I don't know any other life. Out on the street. Mourning and weeping in this valley of tears.' He pauses, pathetic, pleading. 'You wouldn't tell, would you?'

Thomas turns his head to avoid the sight of all this misery.

'What do you mean? Tell the archbishop?' He remembers the traces of tears down the altar boy's cheeks, and feels the surges of repulsion and anger return.

The little priest turns towards him, small eyes wide with another level of fear.

'Of course the archbishop. Who else? Not the police? You wouldn't think of going to the police, would you?' The tears in his eyes spill down his narrow cheeks.

Thomas shifts uncomfortably on the hard kitchen chair. The sight of tears running down the wretched man's face brings tears to his own eyes. How long is it since he has cried? He can't remember. The contempt that has been flooding his mind is, to his own surprise, mixed with a dawning sense of pathos. Will he go to the police? Father Kevin's misery is heart-rending. But there is the little boy. And others too. He can't answer. He can't see far enough ahead to catch any glimpse of exactly what he will do. But whatever it is, he knows he must put a stop to this dreadful story.

He clears his throat, aware that he sounds awkward, uncertain.

'I don't understand. You do this to little boys. Not just this one. Others. For years. But you say Mass every morning, you hear people's confessions, preach sermons, all those other things. How does it fit together? How can you believe in what you do in church, and at the same time go on doing what I've just seen?

Father Kevin looks at the younger man with a puzzled expression.

'What do you mean—what do I believe about what?' There is a growing slur in his voice. Comprehension comes little by little. 'You're asking me whether I believe all that stuff. Is that what you mean? Believe in the body and blood of Christ. Original sin. The Virgin Mary. Purgatory, heaven, hell, all the rest. Is that it?'

He breathes out, a long breath.

'Ah. Now that's something else. Something else entirely.'

The older man stares silently at the empty Vegemite glass on the red Laminex table for a minute or two.

'You want to know something? I've never talked to anyone about this in my life. My whole life. Isn't that peculiar. Never talked about what I believe, what I think—just me, myself.

'You know what it's like. It must have been much the same for you, I suppose. When you're in short pants they send you to the convent. And the Sisters aren't interested in what you believe; they teach you what you have to believe. And you'd better get the answers right when they run a test. So you learn that it's a sin to steal, or miss Mass on Sunday, or eat meat on Friday. Then it's on to the Brothers, and the stuff gets more complicated. Like how much money would you have to steal for it to be a mortal sin instead of a venial sin. Or how far away from the church you'd have to be, to be able to miss Mass on Sunday without committing any sin at all. And it's even more important for your health and safety to get your answers right. Then it's on to the seminary. And eventually you get through to the real technical questions. Like would it be a sin to eat a slice of jam tart on a Friday if there's lard in the pastry, with lard being a meat product? A bit meaty, anyway. Or what happens to babies who die without being baptised? No, that's an easy one. But what would happen if the baby died when the baptism was only half done? Or the priest had a heart attack halfway through and then the baby died?

'Now and then people come to me to ask what they're supposed to believe about stuff like that. You know: what the Church teaches about it. And if I can remember the answer I tell them. If I can't remember I can always look it up in a book.

'Like a woman who came along a few weeks ago. Her husband was the one who jumped off the north wharf down at Fremantle after midnight, with the tide running out. You'd remember the story; it was all over the papers for a few days. Seems he'd lost quite a lot on the horses. She wanted to know whether everyone who committed suicide went to hell, on account of suicide being a mortal sin. Well, I didn't have to look that one up. Explained to her that the only way out was by being insane at the time. But you probably remember that he'd taken off all his clothes before he jumped. Maybe trying to save a few shillings, with his wife being left fairly short. Clothes that someone had drowned in wouldn't be worth a lot, would they? And at the last minute he'd tied his ankles together with a few feet of baler twine in case he tried to swim out in a moment of weakness.

'I told her it looked very much as if he knew what he was doing. So the signs weren't promising. She got quite upset for some reason. Started howling. It wasn't my fault. I don't make the rules; I just tell people what they are.

'I think I've lost my track a bit. What were you asking me? Weren't you wanting to know what I believe—just me? That's a different matter, isn't it?

'Well, what is it that I'm supposed to believe? There's a hell of a lot, isn't there. Even in the basic list. How does it finish? I believe in one holy Catholic and apostolic Church, I acknowledge one baptism for the forgiveness of sins, and I look for the resurrection of the dead and the life of the world to come. That's it, isn't it? Sounds better in Latin.'

Thomas thinks of the creed. For him too it comes more easily in Latin. He listens inside his head to a Gregorian musical setting of the first few lines. Austere music, written in a notation that, like the Latin language, has not been used for centuries outside the Catholic liturgy. He still feels, in spite of the shabby room and the even shabbier situation and the miserable little man sitting opposite, a trace of the sense of being part of this ancient and enclosed tradition, something that lifts him beyond the comprehension of people in the wider world.

Father Kevin stands rather shakily, walks unsteadily to the kitchen sink and props himself up with his hands on the draining board. He speaks, staring out through the window towards the side fence.

'The seminary. You went to Saint Aloysius' I suppose. And then on to Sydney. How old were you at the start?'

Thomas is glad to lose sight of the narrow face and the tear-tracks down the skinny cheeks.

'Me? I was fourteen.' An image forms in his memory, and moves into sharp focus. An image of his arrival at the seminary. He is immature for a fourteen-year-old, conscious at the time of his lack of confidence and ease in company. He walks through an archway into a courtyard enclosed by buildings. He sees unfamiliar people, some boys of about his age, several who look even younger, others who look like men in their twenties or thirties; all dressed in cassocks and clerical collars, and behaving as if they find this quite normal and natural. There is a sensation of panic in his chest as he looks around at the enclosing buildings and the clerical garb, wondering how he came to be in this situation. And how he could get out of it. But he can't see a way out.

Father Kevin picks up his story again.

'Fourteen, for you. With me it was twelve, back in the Old Country. A few other boys the same age, some thirteen, fourteen. As well as us kids there was a batch of grown-up men. They'd probably decided at around twenty-five or thirty that they didn't fit into the ordinary world out there. For one reason or another. Thought they'd try something different.

'So there we were, pitched in together, kids and men. Day and night. Cassocks and clerical collars. Mass, confession, retreats, Gregorian chants. Dormitories, showers. Home for the holidays with the parish priest keeping an eye on you to make sure that your religious vocation was still . . . what's the word? Can't think of it. You probably know what I mean. Intact: that's the word. Untouched. What a laugh. I certainly wasn't untouched.

'One time I remember as if it was last week. I'm home for the holidays. The last holiday before ordination. And I'm afraid. I'm standing in front of the house, wondering whether to go through with it. No, not that: wondering whether to get out of it. No, that's not it either: wondering how to get out of it. And I can't see any way.

'Well, you know what it's like; you're in it yourself. Simple in theory to leave. All you have to do is tell everyone you're getting out, and stick to it. In practice about as simple as standing up in front of everyone at what was supposed to be your wedding, and telling them all that you've changed your mind. Wouldn't go over well. It'd take real guts. More than I had.'

'Anyway, I'm standing outside the house. And there're a few people about my age going down the street. I know they're going to a dance, so it must be Saturday night. I know some of them from childhood. And I'm thinking, that's the ordinary world. That's the world they live in, and I know hardly anything about that world. Been out of it for eleven years. How would I manage? A bit like being dumped in a country where you don't speak the language and they live on raw fish.

'So I decide I might as well go through with it then— ordination I mean. At least it's a job, guaranteed. A place. Jobs weren't so easy to find in them days.'

He turns away from the grimy window, walks unsteadily back to the table, slumps in his chair. The slur is becoming much more obvious in his voice.

'Lost my track again, have I? What were we talking about? That's it—you were asking whether I believe it all.'

There is a long pause. Thomas is beginning to wonder whether the priest has drifted into another foggy detour, but he gropes his way back to the point.

'Never really think about it. Who does? I go through the motions, say the words. They're all in the book; I've got lots of them by heart anyway. Do what's expected. Say what everybody is waiting to hear. Not much call for that sort of thinking in this job. It's already done for us by somebody else.

'What was it again that I was supposed to believe? Those end bits for instance. *I acknowledge one baptism for the forgiveness of sins, and I look for the resurrection of the dead and the life of the world to come.* That's it.'

For a time he is silent, staring down at the table top. Then he looks up into Thomas's face, with the faintest trace of the familiar lop-sided grin.

'Well, not very likely, is it? Seriously. We don't look for the resurrection of dead sheep, do we? Be a bit awkward when we've eaten them, wouldn't it? Nice to imagine that it's different for us, of course. But why would it be? And the forgiveness of sins. Nice to believe that, too. But who's going to forgive some sins? Real sins?

'What about that stuff that comes earlier? Crucified under Pontius Pilate, suffered death, was buried. Third day, rose again, ascended into heaven, right hand of the Father, coming again in glory, and so on. No, I don't think so. Except for the crucified bit. People get crucified all the time, one way or another. Dying too. Everyone does it. Nobody seems to come back. Can't believe any of it, really, apart from one or two bits like that. Not when I look hard at it. Funny, isn't it, me never taking a hard look till now.'

Father Kevin puts both hands to his head, looking down, turning his bald pate towards his listener.

'My head's spinning. The house. Feels like it's going round and round. Got to lie down.' He struggles to his feet and stumbles on a wavering course towards his bedroom.

Thomas, still sitting at the table, stares out through the grimy glass of the kitchen window. He has a sense of looking for something. But what? He's not sure. Almost anything.

Anything different from the deluge of the last few weeks. There's the boundary fence of the church property. Overhanging from the other side is a tall shrub with pink flowers—scores of them. He wonders why he hasn't focused on it before. It's vaguely familiar. A hibiscus, he thinks. That's it: apple blossom hibiscus. He remembers how proud his grandfather was of his, in a corner of the yard down near the back fence. At the old house in the old country town, with the summer-house and the monkey-puzzle tree and the snapdragons at the side, and fruit trees at the back, and behind the fruit trees, the apple blossom hibiscus, always, for him, in bloom.

He stands, moves over to the window, looks past the blossom-laden shrub and over the dividing fence to the backyard of the house next door. The house has a back veranda where a man and a woman are sitting side by side in cane chairs. From their relaxed postures they seem to Thomas to be at ease with each other. There is a fair amount of grey in the hair of both. They are talking about something, but without any appearance of urgency. Their conversation seems to be punctuated from time to time by short periods of silence during one of which Thomas sees the man reach out to touch the woman's arm, and the woman place her hand on his. It is another world.

16

After the Deluge

Thomas sits on the hard, slatted bench under the roof overhang of one of the shelter sheds in the school playground. He's never looked at it before, never noticed what a mean little shed it is, roofed and walled in second-hand material. There's never enough money around a convent school in a parish like this.

One of the boards in the wall has slipped, leaving a gap through which he sees another roof overhang and another bench backing onto his own, no doubt equally hard and uncomfortable.

A distant memory suddenly leaps up: an image that he hasn't thought about for years. He is probably ten years old and is peering through a small gap in another shoddy wall separating the boys' and girls' changing sheds at one of the old swimming spots used by the local kids.

He is watching a girl on the other side who looks to be a couple of years older than him. She is slipping the straps of her bathers off her shoulders, pulling them down, stepping out of them neatly, casually, innocently, without any sense that she might be seen. He watches, tense, trying to breathe silently, waiting for her to turn towards him and reveal—something. He has no idea of what to expect.

But she doesn't turn. She towels the sand off her legs and reaches for her clothes hanging from a peg on the far wall. There are voices outside, coming nearer. He reaches for his own shorts, fumbling to get them on quickly before anyone arrives, looks, sees and guesses.

Thomas turns away from the gap in the school shelter-shed wall, shaking his head to dislodge the image of the straps slipping off the shoulders, the legs stepping neatly out of the bathers, the amazing smoothness of the buttocks and thighs.

As if someone has pressed a switch, a sudden sharply clear series of thoughts lights up in his mind. He has been savouring memories of a naked young girl he watched surreptitiously many years ago. Now he sees himself as if from above, peering secretively with mounting excitement through the sparse stems and leaves of the grass at Jane, as she removes one garment after another. Why does he do these things at twenty-three years of age? It's shameful. How far removed is this from Father Kevin's repulsive behaviour yesterday afternoon? A long way distant, but obviously located in the same direction. The sudden realisation appals him, sets up a nauseous sensation in his belly that rises into his throat.

With an effort Thomas comes back to the present moment, trying to focus on something solid, here and now. Under his feet is the bitumen surface of the cracked and pot-holed school yard. Two or three old stunted pepper trees stand out of the grim black surface, with gnarled trunks and elegant ferny foliage, the school's only gesture towards the world of green, growing things. In front of him is the church of grey concrete blocks and grey asbestos roofing. Beyond the shelter shed are the convent classrooms, built in the same drab grey.

From the end classroom comes the sound of singing: young children's thin voices and uncertain pitch: *Oranges and lemons, say the bells of Saint Clement's, You owe me three farthings, say the bells of Saint Martin's. When will you pay me, say the bells of Old Bailey? When I grow rich, say the bells of Shoreditch.*

The song is suddenly interrupted by a sharp voice with an Irish edge: Sister Agatha.

'Brigid Ryan, you're not singing. Stop daydreaming, girl. Pay attention and join in or you'll feel my stick around your legs. Now. Back to the beginning, and I want to hear everyone this time!'

This time the piping voices get through to the end: *Here comes a candle to light you to bed. Here comes a chopper to chop off your head.*

Now Sister Agatha again.

'Those churches, children. Churches in London. They were all ours once, Catholic churches, every one. The Protestants got them at the time of Henry the Eighth. And they've still got them. But with the help of God and his holy mother they will be ours again one day, when the English return to the true faith.' She sniffs loudly, then adds, 'If that's possible.'

Thomas grins momentarily, listening to the sour note in her voice. She doesn't sound optimistic about the chances of converting the English. Not very enthusiastic about the project either. He remembers a passing comment of Macpherson's about the Irish: *some people seem to need their enemies even more than they need their friends.*

Small children begin straggling out of the school building and spreading in pairs around the yard, under the pepper trees, to the other shelter sheds, to the church steps. Two girls look in at his side of the shed and move on, giggling.

They carry reading books, and the task appears to involve taking turns in hearing each other read. Giggling seems to play a fairly large part in the procedure, too, and Thomas can't help beginning to feel more cheerful.

The most persistent giggling is coming from the other side of the shed. Heartened by the sound of merriment, he slides along the hard bench to look through the strategic gap and discover what is generating it, without interrupting whatever the game is. The pair on the other side are, unusually, a boy and a girl. They are perched on the edge of the hard bench facing each other with no reading books in sight. The skin of their faces, only an arm's length away, has a clean innocent glow to it, in spite of what looks like Vegemite around the boy's mouth. Thomas is struck by their vulnerability. The thought brings up in his mind the shocking image of Father Kevin and his victim, equally vulnerable, from the previous afternoon. With the image comes the same upwelling of repugnance combined with a surge of anger. He forces his attention back to what he is seeing and hearing.

The girl is trying to teach the boy a song. It's one of those repetitive nonsense songs with actions to match the words. He is struggling to follow her lead, his finger going to the wrong part of his body a fair amount of the time, setting off a fresh burst of giggles. *With my hand on my heart, what have I here? This is my nosewiper, my teacher dear. Nosewiper, eyesighter, brainbox and icky dicky dicky doo,* (here they put their thumbs in their ears and flap their fingers), *that's what they taught me when I went to school.*

The song, and the children's hands, work their way down past their chatterboxes, chinwaggers and rubbernecks towards their breadbaskets with many repetitions, numerous mistakes, and much giggling.

In the background from the end schoolroom come snatches of the other song, with an Irish voice in counterpoint. Sister Agatha seems determined to imprint on the children's memories the names of those purloined London churches. *Oranges and lemons say the bells of Saint Clement's, You owe me three farthings, say the bells of Saint Martin's.*

A storm of giggling brings Thomas back to the gap. The pair on the other side have hit on the idea of reversing the song, touching each other in the appropriate places instead of themselves. *This is your chinwagger, my teacher dear. Chinwagger, chatterbox and nosewiper, eyesighter, brainbox and icky dicky dicky doo. That's what they taught me when I went to school.*

They swing into the next verse. *With my hand on your heart, what have you here? This is your rubberneck, oh my teacher dear.* Each has a hand inside the collar of the other's shirt, and the giggling reaches new heights.

The game stops abruptly, cut off by a piercing voice from a classroom window.

'You two! Stop that! Get your hands away from each other's bodies.'

The pair jump apart, look around, eyes wide with fright, and eventually locate Sister Agatha glaring out of the end window.

'Now don't move so much as an inch.'

The pale accusing face disappears from the window and within half a minute the nun is sweeping out of the building and down the few steps, her habit trailing behind. She stands tall over the children. Her eyes are wide. Her face, what can be seen of it that is not concealed by the constricting head-dress, is an even starker white than usual. She is directly in Thomas's view.

'Stand up! What do you think you've been doing?' She grabs each by an ear, pulls them upright, and hauls them around, turning back towards the school building. The boy makes no sound, but the girl whimpers.

'We'll have none of that here. You can stand at the back of my classroom until lunch-time. I'll deal with you then.' She marches them, both flinching, towards the school steps.

Thomas gathers his courage together into a decision and steps out from behind the shelter shed.

'Sister Agatha.'

The nun swings around.

'Surely Sister, there's no need to be so harsh. Those children, they're hardly more than babies. I've been watching them. Listening. They've only been playing. Doing no harm.'

She stares at him for some time without responding. Then she snorts.

'No harm. Is that what you're telling me? You'll excuse me I hope, Mr Riordan, if I point out that I've had more experience with children than you. Original Sin, Mr Riordan. I'm sure I don't have to explain it to you. Young doesn't mean innocent. The triple concupiscence: the three sources of temptation to sin. The world, the flesh and the devil. Especially the flesh.' Somehow she manages to inject a tone of disgust into that last word.

'It's never too early to nip that sort of thing in the bud. Sins against holy purity. Next year they'll both be eight, the age of reason. Capable of mortal sin. Good Catholic parents don't send their children to good Catholic schools to learn behaviour like that.'

Sister Agatha sweeps around again and off towards the school door. Thomas stands by the shed. His initiative has achieved nothing. But at least he has stood up and tried. He hears the yelps of the children as they are dragged up each step. Then the three disappear into the building.

From the church comes the sound of the bell. The Angelus: the midday call to prayer. Father Kevin is going through the motions, as he put it, doing what's expected. Probably repeating the habitual sequence of words. *Angelus domini . . . The angel of the lord declared unto Mary; and she conceived by the Holy Ghost . . . Pray for us sinners now and at the hour of our death.* The traditional plea for help. But what if there is nobody out there to hear it?

Startled, Thomas focuses on that unpremeditated thought. What if there is nobody there to hear? Is it possible that the ritual words are projected out into a void where there is nobody listening? Where has this shocking question come from? Why does it break through into his consciousness at this moment? He tries to push it out of focus and back into a corner where it can be ignored, at least for the present. But he knows that it has found a foothold. However hard he tries to redirect his attention, it will be back sooner or later, demanding that he confront it.

He turns to wondering what thoughts might be moving in the small priest's mind under the tolling bell and the unthinking words. Surely he must be filled with anxiety about the previous afternoon and the possible looming consequences. More than anxiety. Fear. How can he be slipping into the familiar daily routine as if nothing significant has happened? Surely he has some sense of the enormity of what he was seen doing. Waves of nausea overtake Thomas as the scene witnessed through that front room window comes back to him. He realises that he's been avoiding the issue—trying to focus on other things. But he is also aware that the time for decisive action is looming. How many times has the Regan boy been subjected to that outrage? And how many other defenceless little boys?

The Angelus bell rings on towards the end of the ritual sequence. Thomas imagines the short, ageing man standing on the porch, pulling the bell-rope, his lips moving as he mouths the ritual words. Another disturbing thought intrudes. He imagines himself in ten years, twenty years, thirty. Will his life, like Father Kevin's, be centred on going through the ritual motions, repeating the ritual words? Is this really what God wants of him? The question is immediately overwhelmed by the other terrifying question. Is it possible, is it even thinkable, that there is really no God to hear, to see, to want anything of him?

Can it be, that he has been living inside a complicated edifice of myths and rules and rituals, without any foundations? An intricate fabrication? And perhaps not altogether an innocent one. What did Macpherson say? *An inhuman streak. And sometimes perverted.*

Perverted. How far might Thomas himself drift in the same direction as Father Kevin if he continues to allow the same current to carry him along? He recalls his memory of the young naked girl in the changing shed—his horror at the thought that he has floated even a short distance that way.

A huge wave of questions is breaking over his head. And he is floundering among them; drowning in challenges that demand to be confronted. He suddenly feels a dizzying sensation of vertigo as if he were spiralling down into empty space.

He half closes his eyes and lets their focus drift out past Saint Brigid's to bring up from his memory the reassuring image of the real church that stands behind it. And a trace of it is still there: at least, a very hazy outline of the splendid structure of pale golden stone, with soaring spires, fanciful gargoyles and saints looking out from the carved niches and the stained glass of the windows. But it's much further away, the details much vaguer than when he last conjured it up. The image is fading. Whatever music is perhaps being sung inside is far beyond his hearing.

Children's voices from the end classroom come to him again. *Today or tomorrow, say the bells of Saint Sorrow.'* Thomas senses the approach of another thought. It's nothing sharply defined, only the hazy outline of a realisation away in the distance. But with it comes a feeling that he is caught up in a different current that is inevitably drifting him in a new direction, sweeping him closer to an idea not yet properly in sight, bringing that thought, in time, more clearly into view. The realisation that someday soon, today or tomorrow, or perhaps next week or next month, he will search his memory and the image will be gone. And with it, the whole elaborate fantasy that lies behind this fading image of the spires, the saints' statues, the brilliant windows—all gone.

Melted into air, into thin air. Where did that line come from? Shakespeare again, probably. The rector was very determined about Shakespeare. About literature in general. Though he never seemed to get any pleasure from it. Or from anything else either.

Into thin air. And there will be nothing left except that ugly grey shed of a church and Sister Agatha hauling children around by their ears, and Father Kevin going through the motions and harrying his flock about the parish debt, and much worse. And if there's nothing else left, what then? Perhaps there will be something else after all, but for the moment he can't see what it might be.

Thomas turns away to the problem of the moment. What about Father Kevin and the Regan boy? The unavoidable conclusion emerges ready-made from the recesses of his mind. Like the unexplained disappearance of a young lady, this is not the archbishop's business; it is police business. The archbishop might, in spite of Father Kevin's fears, simply move him on to another parish, as the previous incumbent had done, several times. Of course Thomas must go to the police with his story. And of course the consequences for Father Kevin will be dire, with an adult eyewitness testifying to what he saw. He can see the tears spilling down the old man's cheeks. But there is no possible alternative.

The consequences for Thomas himself, these are more difficult to think about. Going to the police will surely be seen as treachery. He will be cutting himself off from the world he has lived in for years. But that world of the imagination, with its spires and saints and stained glass and Latin plain-chant, has already faded. For him it will be completely gone soon, he realises, no matter what he does about Father Kevin. And he will have to look for another world. He has no idea what else he is likely to find there.

He wanders past the church towards the presbytery, and beyond it, the boundary of the church property. There is that shrub leaning over from the other side of the fence. Apple blossom hibiscus. Pink flowers covering it. So many have fallen that there's a fading carpet of blossom covering a patch of the otherwise barren ground. To have a shrub like that would be worth something. It wouldn't last forever; but perhaps nothing does.

17

Another World

Tom wakes again suddenly, out of the same dream. It has been waiting for him in ambush for weeks, emerging at least once, sometimes twice a night; one night it came three times. In the dream he is swimming in a huge expanse of dark water. He sees her in the water, too. He is conscious in the dream that it is some time since she was with him, but she is there, a long way off, and swimming steadily towards him. He sets out to swim to her, to touch her, to hold her. They approach closer and closer until both are stretching out arms to each other and their hands are almost touching. And he wakes, stretching out his arm to touch her, hold her, finding again her absence in the empty bed.

Sleep has become even more difficult. He goes to bed every night afraid of the dream hiding there in wait for him, and the desolate awakening. What sleep he gets seems to leave him feeling more exhausted than before.

Everyone has good advice to offer. Time, they say, will make it easier; they don't explain how much more of it is needed. Time moves at its own pace.

Try to remember the good times—that is another piece of advice that he hears everywhere. He thinks of a good time. Calls up a cherished memory of her walking towards him naked out of the water on a secluded beach. One of their many camping trips. Tears come to his eyes with the thought that a time like that will not come again.

She laughs, asks him whether he ever imagined himself naked on a beach with a naked woman during all those years when he was studying to be a priest. She's never understood how he could have given even a moment to considering that as a plan for life. Even if he was only thirteen or fourteen at the beginning. He must have wanted to feel important. Like all those priests up there in pulpits, telling everyone who'll listen about how to live their lives. How on earth would they know, when they've cut themselves off from most of life? Like men and women coming together, as he and she have done. And feeding the kids and giving them a hug at bed-time, and getting up in the middle of the night to change the baby's nappy. Things like that keep the world turning, as everyone who's involved in them would know. Not spires and church windows and imaginary angels and saints and chanting in a language hardly anyone understands. How could he be taken in by that fantasy for so long?

She could be like that—confronting him with forthright, challenging questions while standing naked on a beach. He could find no response that satisfied her. Or that really satisfied him either. How is he going to live from this time on?

Behind her, behind the memory of her standing on the beach, appears an image of another beach, even more remote in time and space, with, away in the distance, another human figure. Another young woman. And waves breaking on a reef of dark rock, and a channel of water sheltered by the dark reef with a line of foam running through it.

He shakes his head, trying to dissipate the black fog that has settled over him. Realising that something more decisive is needed to break the mood, he decides to walk down to the beach for an early morning swim.

It's a short walk, only a quarter of an hour at the sort of brisk pace he needs to set in order to get a bit more life and light into his legs and his thoughts. Tom finds himself thinking about the couples in the houses he passes on the way, in bed still, most of them, at this time of the morning, pressed against the comfort of each other's bodies. Not all of them, he supposes. He and she had been lucky. In most ways.

The beach is deserted. The tide has retreated, leaving a strip of sand washed clear of yesterday's footprints. His own prints are the first of the new day. There is a small pleasure in that. He drops towel and thongs on the sand and wades into the water.

It's another windless morning. The sun has not long cleared the horizon and the glare is reflected off the glassy surface, dazzling him when he looks back. There is still nobody else on the beach. He turns away from the harsh light and plunges in, swimming away from the shore.

He's unfit and out of practice. It's not as easy as it used to be to control his stroke and his kick and his breathing into a steady rhythm. He can already feel the strain in muscles that have not had enough use for months, for years. But he swims on.

He's panting when he slows his pace and stops for a rest, treading water as he looks back towards the empty beach.

How far? Maybe a couple of hundred yards. Probably a bit less. He turns away again from the sun.

Underwater, the ocean is dark. At such a shallow angle, the sunlight is barely penetrating the surface. He can make out the indistinct mass of a reef about ten or twelve feet down, and on the seaward side of it, a drop-off into deeper water. The surfaces of the reef are covered with a dense growth of seaweed like a dim, shadowy forest.

He lifts his head to breathe, thinking about the wretched priest standing on the edge of the wharf at Fremantle, looking down into dark murky water, taking a breath while he can, and then another, holding off the unthinkable moment when breathing will stop, trying to build up enough courage for the final plunge. Did he regret the decision later? A pointless question; he was not there later to regret it. What was left of him was buried, of course, in the Catholic section at Karrakatta Cemetery. Was that really Father Kevin? He had simply ceased to exist. He was nowhere. He had surely been right about that when he had finally got around to looking hard at it: no resurrection, no life everlasting, either for punishment or reward. *Macbeth* comes back into Tom's mind. A dark play. *Duncan is in his grave. After life's fitful fever he sleeps well.*

Father Kevin is in his grave. Does he sleep well? Tom is not sleeping well. It's his sleep, not his waking, that's fitful, interrupted, filled with disturbing dreams, haunted by the fear of waking to the pain of loss. The priest will not wake at all, of course. Nobody else will either. But who would want to wake to more pain? A deep dreamless sleep without any looming fear of waking, ever—the image does something to blur the sharp edges of reality. There must be millions of tombstones in thousands of cemeteries inscribed with the words *Sleeping Peacefully*. The living softening the thought of the death of someone they have loved, making it a little more bearable. And perhaps, unconsciously, looking towards their own deaths through the same consoling lens. *Sleeping Peacefully*. In the end what else could anyone look for?

His legs are beginning to feel chilled, stiff from the cold and the unaccustomed exercise. It's time he was heading back to the beach before they begin to cramp. Instead he decides to swim a little further out to sea before turning back. He doesn't examine the quick decision to ask himself what it means.

He swims out slowly but steadily. There's another fragment of verse stirring in a back corner of his memory, but it's not coming into view yet.

He thinks about a conversation with her, many years before, fairly early in their marriage. He can picture her standing at the kitchen table sketching out on a piece of cloth a part of the tiny nightie that she was making for the baby who was due two months later.

They had been talking about Father Kevin's end, and about the man who had taken exactly the same way out only a few months before him. She wanted to know what the Catholic Church had to say about suicide. As a recent and well-informed ex-member, he was ready with an answer. Suicide was classed as a major sin. Possibly the gravest sin of all. And when she asked about sins, he produced the school catechism definition of them as offences against the law of God.

Her reaction was surprisingly quick and passionate. *That's all nonsense, isn't it? Beside the point. What harm would suicide do to God, for him to have made a law banning it? That is assuming that there is a God. The question is, what it does to the people who are left behind. With someone like that miserable priest, maybe that wasn't a problem. Did anyone cry at his funeral? There might have been a few people who were pleased to know that he'd gone, from what she's heard about him. The other fellow, he was a different case. He had a wife. He'd promised to love her. There were probably children, too. What was he doing to them? He was walking out on all his commitments. All his promises. Pure selfishness. Surely nobody needs to imagine a God to see what's wrong with that.*

All these years later, he can still picture her turning back to her task, picking up the pattern book, smiling down at the baby in the illustration—imagining no doubt, her own baby dressed in the tiny garment she was making.

He has stopped swimming, holding the memory close, thinking about what she said. Walking out on all his commitments. He's promised to go to his daughter's for tea tonight—the same daughter for whom that tiny nightie was being made over forty years ago. And he has made a commitment to look after her dog for a few days next month. Other things too, for other people. Trivial promises maybe; the time for the big promises that shape a life is long gone. But there are still small fragments left of what keeps the world turning.

He turns back towards the shore, looking briefly down into the shadowy depths of the water and the dim masses of reef and seaweed, thinking, again, about Father Kevin. And Jane, whose body was never found on that far-away beach so long ago. And now that other once-young woman for whom he still reaches out, waking in the empty bed. All sleeping peacefully. The fragment of verse that has been stirring at the back of his memory finally steps out of the shadows.

The woods are lovely, dark and deep,
But I have promises to keep,
And miles to go before I sleep.
And miles to go before I sleep.

He faces into the sunlight and strikes out for the shore.